White Buffalo

A Play in Two Acts

by
Don Zolidis

SAMUEL FRENCH, INC.

45 West 25th Street
NEW YORK 10010
LONDON

7623 Sunset Boulevard
HOLLYWOOD 90046
TORONTO

IMPORTANT BILLING AND CREDIT REQUIREMENTS

CAST OF CHARACTERS

CAROL GELLING, 40, a robust and energetic woman. Still attractive, but beginning to show her age.

MIKE GELLING, 41, Carol's ex-husband. Wiry and tough, but gentle.

ABBY GELLING, 18, their daughter, a very intelligent and attractive young woman who has been experimenting with the counterculture.

JOHN TWO RIVERS, 24, a young Lakota Sioux businessman from Chicago.

ANDERSON WILKES, 50s, owner of a large ranch out west.

CHORUS, consisting of four members who play various roles throughout the play. They are referred to as FIRST MAN, FIRST WOMAN, FIRST BOY, and FIRST GIRL. Although the actors playing boy and girl should be younger, they do not need to be children. The Chorus members should be Native Americans, and are responsible for all the music in the play. When singing or playing instruments, they should be visible to the audience unless otherwise noted.

SETTING

The Gelling farm, just south of Blackhawk, Wisconsin, close to the Illinois border.

TIME
The present. Late summer.

Note: The main event described in this play, the birth of a white buffalo calf, occurred in Janesville, Wisconsin in 1994. The myths and legends associated with it, as well as their importance to many tribes, are true. All other events in this play and all characters within it, however, are purely fiction.

ACT I

*(Scene one. The Gelling farm and environs. On stage is a
cross-section of a farm house and its adjoining field. The house
is a rather cramped structure from the turn of the century, lov-
ingly maintained, but succumbing to decay and ruin. The paint
is beginning to peel, the wood is largely warped, and the fields
are fallow. The living room and kitchen are the only rooms visible to the audience. A set of stairs leads up to a second story
off-stage, and a small door leads to the basement. The living
room is rather dark, but simple. Clearly, this is the most lived-
in room of the house, and all manner of pictures, family albums
and knickknacks abound on various bookshelves. A small television is located against one wall, but it is clearly not the focus
of the room. Numerous water-damaged boxes cluster near the
basement door, some half-opened. The kitchen is quite small
and old-fashioned and contains one small table where most
meals are eaten, and is otherwise stuffed with heirlooms and a
seemingly inexhaustible supply of pots and pans. A screen door
leads out back to the field, which is mostly a path of dirt punc-
tuated by a few clumps of scraggly grass. Far upstage is a large
wooden fence, which pens in the animals beyond. NOTE: In
several places in the play, it must be clear the action is not taking place in the literal confines of the set stage, but rather in a
metaphorical setting. In order to accomplish this, there must be
some type of large open area that might be carved out with light*

WHITE BUFFALO

or likewise delineated as not part of the "real world."
At rise, the stage is backlit, rendering the frame of the house and
fence into silhouette. A single flute intones a soft swirl, and then
is accompanied by a single, powerful male voice. The man chants
a slow and mournful series of notes, then falls silent. SPOT-
LIGHT on JOHN TWO RIVERS, an attractive Native American
man in his early twenties. He wears an expensive suit and tie
and has his hair cut short. He stands momentarily near the fence,
unsure of where he is, briefcase in hand. There is a moment of
silence before the voice begins again. JOHN looks for the source
of it, but cannot find it. The flute begins again, and the first
voice is joined by a younger voice. As JOHN backs away, the
FIRST MAN becomes visible as a silhouette standing on top of
the fence. When fully visible, he appears to be a Sioux man of
indeterminate age dressed in traditional clothing. JOHN ap-
proaches him cautiously, and the voices fall silent. A drum beat
begins, slowly gaining speed and intensity, accompanied by the
sounds of a storm. A burst of lightning illuminates the FIRST
MAN's face and reveals the other members of the chorus, emerg-
ing from the four cardinal points of the stage. All of them are
beginning to close in on JOHN. JOHN spins around, confused,
as all the members of the chorus begin to sing. They close in on
him, and drums from off-stage join the sound. Their chant grows
louder and more intense, and the drums rise in power to match
their voices, sounding almost like a stampeding herd. Thunder
and lightning join in with them. Abruptly, the chanting and drums
stop. As one, the CHOURS members seize JOHN and lift him
off the ground. He is lifted over the fence and held by the FIRST
MAN.)

FIRST MAN. See
FIRST WOMAN. See

WHITE BUFFALO

FIRST BOY. See
FIRST GIRL. See

(A soft white light begins to glow from off-stage in the field. It grows brighter as the CHORUS continues to speak.)

FIRST MAN. See
FIRST WOMAN. It begins
FIRST BOY. She is born
FIRST GIRL. She returns
FIRST MAN. He lays down his life
FIRST WOMAN. He dies
FIRST BOY. For Her
FIRST GIRL. For her return

(They continue to say these lines, overlapping each other as the light grows brighter and brighter. All silent as the light washes out the stage.)

FIRST WOMAN. It begins.

(Blackout, and the sounds of the storm give way to birds chirping. The lights come up slowly on the interior of the house, early in the morning. The first light of dawn appears faintly in the east. CAROL opens the screen door and walks out of the kitchen, sitting down on the outside step. She carries her mud-caked boots with her. As she unlaces them, FIRST WOMAN appears directly upstage. She plays the flute quietly and serenely. CAROL takes no notice of this. When CAROL has her second boot on, FIRST BOY appears stage left, near the barn. He plays a quiet beat on the drums. CAROL finishes with her boots, stands up, and stretches. She takes a large bag of feed from the barn and

heads to the fence, slowly and carefully emptying the bag into the troughs attached to the fence. As she does this, FIRST GIRL appears stage right, close to the front of the house. She plays the flute in a quicker rhythm than the mother. Once CAROL finishes with the food, she stops for a second, looks out into the field and freezes—all music and sound, including the birds, stops suddenly. CAROL, her attention still focused on the field, rushes back to the barn and puts the bag down. The FIRST MAN appears, sitting downstage. He speaks to the air.)

FIRST MAN. She sees. *(CAROL opens the gate slowly. Still no sound.)* She walks into the field.
FIRST WOMAN. She sees. *(CAROL steps into the field.)* She walks into the field.
FIRST MAN. The grass is wet with dew. The sun sparkles in its water—
FIRST WOMAN. The clouds swirl near the edge of the sky—
FIRST BOY. The air sings—
FIRST MAN. It is cool on her skin.

(CAROL continues to walk, slightly quicker now, emerging from the area behind the fence into the "field," which should be directly centered between the four members of the CHORUS. FIRST GIRL begins to play the flute again, slowly now.)

FIRST WOMAN. She sees
FIRST MAN. She sees
FIRST BOY. She sees
FIRST MAN. The buffalo stand beneath a row of trees—
FIRST WOMAN. *(Overlapping.)* Then she sees her—
FIRST MAN. *(Overlapping.)* Something strange—

WHITE BUFFALO

FIRST BOY. *(Overlapping.)* Some of the buffalo still sleep—
FIRST MAN. *(Overlapping.)* There she is.

(FIRST GIRL, continuing to play the flute, sheds her outer coat, revealing a suit of pure white beneath. She steps into the center of the stage.)

FIRST WOMAN. Next to her mother.

(The FIRST WOMAN walks downstage to meet the FIRST GIRL. They both look directly at CAROL.)

FIRST MAN. They stand together—mother and child—
FIRST WOMAN. The calf—
FIRST BOY. *(Overlapping.)* The calf—
FIRST MAN *(Overlapping.)* The calf—pure white—with dark shining eyes—pressed against her mother—
FIRST WOMAN *(Overlapping.)* She has come—
FIRST BOY (overlapping) She is here—
FIRST MAN. *(Overlapping.)* She has returned.

(Brief pause. They now describe CAROL.)

FIRST WOMAN. She stands.
FIRST BOY. She watches.

(CAROL takes a step back.)

FIRST MAN. She feels it.
FIRST WOMAN. She feels—

(The FIRST BOY plays the drum like a slow heartbeat.)

FIRST MAN. She feels.

CAROL. *(Shouting out.)* Abby! Abby! Come out here! *(CAROL dashes off the way she came. The CHORUS scatters as CAROL runs from the field, comes back through the fence and up to the screen door. She opens it and runs inside, not bothering to take off her boots.)* Abby! You gotta see this! *(CAROL jumps up the stairs in the living room. She comes back quickly, bewildered.)* Abby? *(Lights fade on the house and remain on the field for a moment. The FIRST MAN plays a slow series of notes on the flute. The lights come down on him as he sings the same refrain from the beginning of the play.)*

(Lights switch to mid-afternoon. The front door opens slowly as ABBY creeps in. She's carrying a backpack and looks bedraggled. She takes a furtive glance around the living room, then dashes up the stairs.)

CAROL. *(From above.)* Aha!

ABBY. *(Above.)* Ah! Jesus! What the hell are you doing?!

(ABBY scoots back down the stairs with CAROL close on her heels.)

CAROL. Where were you last night?

ABBY. I fell asleep over at Debbie's. I called—

CAROL. You called at eleven to say you were gonna be late.

ABBY. Right.

CAROL. It's one o' clock in the afternoon.

ABBY. Yeah, late. Very late. What the hell is going on in the living room?

CAROL. The basement flooded.

ABBY. It didn't even rain that much last night—

CAROL. Well imagine my surprise then at finding the basement under two feet of water. I've been working at this since seven—

ABBY. Then what were you doing lying in wait for me at the top of the stairs?

CAROL. I was taking a break.

ABBY. Nice, Mom. Real nice. I'm going to Madison tonight, by the way. *(CAROL looks at her.)* What?

CAROL. What do you think?

ABBY. That I'm going to Madison tonight?

CAROL. Try again.

ABBY. That I'm going to Madison tonight?

CAROL. Look at this! I need you to help me clean out the basement—

ABBY. How long is that gonna take?

CAROL. Until we're both dead. And there's a whole lot of other things around here that need doing—you need to sweep out the barn, you need to feed the animals, I did it for you this morning, but they need it this afternoon—

ABBY. Well how bout I—

CAROL. How bout you go downstairs and pull up the rest of the boxes?

ABBY. Can I go to Madison after I'm done?

CAROL. What's in Madison?

ABBY. The State Capitol. A fine library system.

CAROL. No.

ABBY. How bout—

CAROL. Abby. Will you please go downstairs and bring up the rest of the boxes?

ABBY. Fine. *(ABBY opens the door to the basement.)* You know, I thought this was America. I thought we had freedom—

CAROL. *(Interrupting.)* Oh shut up—

ABBY. *(Continuing as she heads down the stairs.)* Instead, I live under an oppressive autocratic regime where—God, it's gross down here!

    CAROL. *(Calling.)* Just get the ones that aren't completely soaked!

(CAROL goes to the boxes in the living room and continues to save items from the wreck, work she has clearly been at for some time. We continue to hear ABBY complain about the disaster in the basement.)

    ABBY. *(From below.)* Do we want these carpets!
    CAROL. *(Calling.)* No! Get the boxes!

(ABBY comes up momentarily carrying a large, extremely water-damaged box. As soon as she gets up the stairs, the bottom rips through and its contents flop to the ground.)

    ABBY. Shit.
    CAROL. Hey.
    ABBY. Why is it every time I come home you have something absolutely disgusting for me to do?
    CAROL. Cause I want to see you suffer.
    ABBY. Oh God— *(She begins sifting through the things—she pulls something, gigantic, hairy, and sopping wet out of the mess.)* Oh God there's like a dead rat or something—
    CAROL. What? *(ABBY holds it up gingerly.)* That's a wig.
    ABBY. Why?
    CAROL. People wore wigs. They were stylish.
    ABBY. I guess.

(ABBY flings it against the wall.)

    CAROL. Could you please just... not cause more damage?

ABBY. Fine. What is all this crap anyway?

CAROL. I don't know. Some of it's your father's—

ABBY. What does he have stuff here for?

CAROL. I don't know. *(CAROL pulls out an outrageous disco shirt from the '70s.)* Here we go.

ABBY. That's awesome.

CAROL. We should find a stash of fake gold chains any minute now.

ABBY. Can I have that?

CAROL. No.

ABBY. Oh come on—

CAROL. These need to be burned.

ABBY. Aw these are cute— *(ABBY pulls out some baby clothes.)* Were these mine?

CAROL. No those were Trevor's.

ABBY. Oh.

CAROL. I was going to take them to the Salvation Army a long time ago... I guess I didn't get to it.

ABBY. Yeah.

CAROL. Did you happen to go to Blackhawk Tech yesterday?

ABBY. No.

CAROL. You need to get that application in.

ABBY. You've only told me that twelve times—

CAROL. Well—do you know when the deadline is?

ABBY. Mom—come on, I'm not going to Blackhawk Technical College. Please. It's one step above Middle School. There's an entire class in how to balance your checkbook.

CAROL. Well I'm just saying that—

ABBY. It might even be a major.

CAROL. It's something, isn't it?

ABBY. So?

CAROL. I'm not gonna do this for you—

ABBY. I realize that.

CAROL. And I still don't understand how you couldn't find it in your heart to attend classes in the spring cause you had that scholarship all lined up—

ABBY. I know.

CAROL. I mean it's like three months of school, Abby—everyone manages to get through it. But suddenly you go and develop an aversion to having a brain—

ABBY. All right, all right.

CAROL. You got into a good college—

ABBY. How many times do I gotta hear it? Just tell me. Like fifteen? Twenty? What's the number? I just want to go write it down so I know.

CAROL. Well then don't complain about Blackhawk Tech. *(They work. ABBY seethes. Pause.)*

CAROL. Sue had her calf this morning.

ABBY. Really?

CAROL. It's really weird.

ABBY. What is?

CAROL. The calf.

ABBY. What's wrong with it?

CAROL. It's white. I mean it's like... snow white.

ABBY. Is it an albino?

CAROL. No, I don't—it's just—it's white. You need to go see her, it's pretty cool actually. Big Ralph's not doing well though.

ABBY. Oh—I should go check on him.

(She gets up.)

CAROL. You don't have to check on him now.

ABBY. More fun than sitting here.

WHITE BUFFALO

(ABBY heads out toward the fence—flute music plays softly.)

ABBY. *(Spots something and stops.)* Wow. *(The music rises as the lights switch. The FIRST GIRL, still dressed in white, appears beyond the fence in very faint light. She stands next to the FIRST WOMAN, in much the same way as they appeared earlier. For a moment they are alone with the music, before the FIRST MAN appears center-stage. He sings very slowly, sinking to his knees. ABBY sees him, and approaches cautiously. The FIRST MAN, obviously in pain, continues to sink lower. ABBY sits next to him and watches as the lights slowly fade.*

(CAROL is heard on the phone abruptly.)

CAROL. *(Into phone.)* If you could come out this afternoon that would be great. I can't move him, he's just too big. Right. Right. *(Lights come back up on the house in the daytime. CAROL is on a corded phone in the kitchen.)* He's in the trees out back, we can probably get the truck out there, but I just don't know how to lift him into the bed of it. I mean, he's like a thousand pounds. He's huge. Yeah, I guess that might work. I don't know, my ex-husband always handled this beforehand, we haven't had one die in close to ten years—*(JOHN approaches the front door during this conversation, dressed in a suit. He has a newspaper in his hand. He looks around for a minute, then presses the doorbell. Nothing happens. He tries it again, looking in through the window. Again, nothing happens. He knocks on the door.)* He seemed healthy enough until this week, and then he just—oh wait, the guy for the foundation is here, hold on one second. *(She calls upstairs)* Abby can you get the door!
    ABBY. *(From above.)* I'm busy!
    CAROL. Will you please get the door I'm on the phone!

ABBY. *(Upstairs.)* This is why we need a new phone!
CAROL. Please!

(ABBY comes down the stairs as CAROL continues speaking into the phone.)

ABBY. You know everyone in the whole world has a cordless phone and we just sit here with this Alexander Graham Bell model from 1902—
CAROL. *(Into phone.)* Sorry about that—our basement flooded last week so that's still a big mess and—

(ABBY opens the front door just as JOHN is about to knock again.)

ABBY. *(To JOHN.)* Hi.
JOHN. Is this the Gelling residence?
ABBY. Yep. Are you here about the foundation? I'm guessing no.
JOHN. What foundation?
ABBY. To the house.
JOHN. No. My name's John—I... uh... saw this in the paper today?

(He holds up an unimportant-looking page of the local newspaper— ABBY looks at it.)

ABBY. Mom, there's a guy from the newspaper here.
JOHN. No, I just saw this in the paper. Is this your buffalo?
ABBY. Yeah. *(ABBY takes the paper.)* I didn't know this was gonna be in the paper—this is so cool. My Mom must have sent this in.
JOHN. Has anyone else been out here?

WHITE BUFFALO

ABBY. For what?
JOHN. To see the buffalo?
ABBY. No... who are you again?

(CAROL is getting off the phone.)

CAROL. *(Into the phone.)* Great. Thanks so much. I'll see you this afternoon then.

(She hangs up and heads toward the living room.)

JOHN. My name is John Two Rivers, I'm from Chicago, well not really, but... I'm Sioux, Lakota actually, and I had a dream, a vision—
CAROL. Wait, what's going on?
JOHN. I'm not explaining this well. I saw this here in the paper and—can I go look at the calf?
CAROL. Why?
JOHN. I just... *(A flute is heard in the distance.)* I just want to see.
CAROL. We're not really selling them.
JOHN. No I just want to see if this is real.
ABBY. O-kay. I mean we're not really in the business of fabricating buffalo photos, but...
CAROL. I'm Carol by the way— *(She shakes hands with him.)* This is Abby—We can go have a look. So are you like scientifically interested in this—I didn't really know that buffalo came in white— I've never really seen one before—here we'll go around the outside.

(CAROL leads JOHN around the outside of the house toward the fence. ABBY follows.)

JOHN. I've never seen one before either—they're extremely rare.

ABBY. Are you like a buffalo expert?

JOHN. No, it's more of a cultural interest—

CAROL. Well we don't have much of a herd out here—we've got a few other animals, but uh... *(They reach the fence.)* You know we just keep the bison around cause we like 'em, frankly. We were gonna sell them for meat back before—*(JOHN is no longer paying any attention to her.)* At first I thought a cow had wandered in— *(More flute music in the distance.)*

JOHN. Her father... is dead?

CAROL. *(Perplexed.)* Yeah.

ABBY. He died this morning.

JOHN. Stomach problem?

ABBY. How do you know that?

JOHN. I've seen this before. In a dream. I uh... no one has come out here?

CAROL. No, what's going on?

JOHN. Do you know the significance of this?

CAROL. No.

JOHN. A white buffalo is the most sacred thing you could ever find.

ABBY. Really?

JOHN. And there hasn't been one born in... in generations. And a female calf—to have a white female calf born... it's like uh... it's everything.

CAROL. What do you mean, everything?

JOHN. My people—the Sioux—among many others—many tribes, believe... in a legend—that's central to our—to their... to their knowledge of who they are. There's a prophecy too—

(Lights begin to shift on stage. A flute plays.)

WHITE BUFFALO

ABBY. What's the legend?

JOHN. I haven't thought about this in a long time, but... It goes—in the days before horses, there was a time of great suffering on the plains. There was no food for anyone, and all the people were starving—so two young men, brothers, went out to hunt—*(The FIRST MAN and FIRST BOY appear, dressed as hunters.)* And they searched for many days, but they found nothing. And on the third day, when they were about to give up their search, a woman appeared to them—*(Accompanied by the fanfare of music, the FIRST WOMAN, dressed all in white as the WHITE BUFFALO WOMAN, appears before the two men.)* She was the most beautiful woman they had ever seen, and she was dressed all in white, the purest white you could imagine. One of the brothers *(The FIRST MAN tries to approach her; he reaches out to grasp her, but she eludes him. Drums pound and he falls away.)* saw her and knew lust in his heart. He reached out to possess her, and was consumed by the air, transformed into a pile of bones. To the other, who showed no desire—

WHITE BUFFALO WOMAN. Go back to your people. Tell them I have come for them. They need fear no longer. Take this, and you shall become a prayer on this Earth. *(She hands him a small package. The hunter unwraps it and sees a long pipe. He bows to her, and departs. The WHITE BUFFALO WOMAN steps forward, accompanied by strong music. She approaches JOHN.)* You are children of the land. You come from the ground beneath your feet and the air that fills your lungs. You are the same as the clouds and stars, from the deep-flowing rivers to the high hills. You are all a part of the sacred hoop of life.

JOHN. And with her came the buffalo, who saved our people from starvation. She taught us how to use them, and she taught us ceremonies and mysteries—but she stayed only a few days—*(She turns her back on JOHN.)*

WHITE BUFFALO

WHITE BUFFALO WOMAN. When I am needed most, in another time of great turmoil, I shall return to you and all the children of the earth. My sign will be a white buffalo calf—

JOHN. And as she left, she appeared in the form of a white buffalo. And as the people watched, she transformed from white to red to yellow and then black, before finally turning the most brilliant shade of white they had ever seen.

(The WHITE BUFFALO WOMAN disappears.)

CAROL. Wow.

JOHN. And the prophecy says that the appearance of a white buffalo calf foretells a time of peace and unity among all people of all colors. This is what the Sioux believe. And there are dozens of other tribes with similar stories.

CAROL. Wow.

ABBY. So this is like peace on earth? *(He nods.)* Right here, right now?

JOHN. So the legend says.

ABBY. Dude. *(Short pause.)* So I mean is that her—I mean, literally, is that the white buffalo woman?

JOHN. Many people would probably believe that. So what you have here, according to my people at least, is the savior of the world.

(Pause. Lights shift. Broadcast static is audible, which quickly separates into the intermingling din of radio and television broadcasts. Voices are discernable for a brief moment, then fade back into the confusion. ABBY, CAROL, and JOHN remain on stage, greeting the CHORUS members as they arrive, laden with gifts and artwork. Throughout this next scene, the CHORUS will begin to adorn the area in front of the fence with pieces of art, votive candles, and numerous homemade crafts. They will

continue to do this for the rest of the first act so that by the beginning of the second act, the entire expanse of the fence will be covered in artwork.)

VOICE #1. Her mother might weigh twelve hundred pounds, but this bundle of joy is believed to be the reincarnation of an ancient spirit—
VOICE #2. The small town of Blackhawk, Wisconsin, home to twenty thousand people, an automotive plant, and now, a miracle.

(The FIRST MAN nearly runs up to CAROL and embraces her in a gigantic bear hug, lifting her off the ground.)

VOICE #3. Her name is Hope, and she represents—

(ANDERSON WILKES, a middle-aged white man, arrives near the back of the CHORUS. He greets CAROL happily and shakes her hand vigorously before joining the others.)

VOICE #4. They have come from all over just to see—
VOICE #5. According to the National Buffalo Association, the odds of a white buffalo are close to six billion to one—

(The FIRST MAN speaks as if he were giving an interview.)

FIRST MAN. It will be a time of peace. For all people. Red, White, Black, and Yellow. This is like the Second Coming of Christ—
FIRST WOMAN. I was sitting in my office in DC when I heard the news. I got a phone call from my sister who said she heard on the news that there was a White Buffalo born in Wisconsin—I couldn't believe it. I cried. And I had to come out, I had to see her, so many people have been waiting so long for this—

FIRST MAN. *(Overlapping.)* This is a sign of the rebirth of our spirituality, of our belief—

WILKES. *(Overlapping.)* Well I just couldn't believe it when I heard the news—

FIRST GIRL. *(Overlapping.)* —And I had to sit in the car for ten hours. Ten hours. You have no idea how boring South Dakota is until you've been driving on I-90 for ten hours—

FIRST WOMAN. *(Overlapping.)* I called my mother in Montana. I haven't seen her in five years—and I thought we should meet out here—

WLIKES. *(Overlapping.)* I got on the first plane. I mean, this is the kind of thing that you never expect to happen in your lifetime—you know, a myth, that becomes reality—

FIRST MAN. *(Overlapping.)* I think people are so interested in Native American beliefs because of the suffering in the world—and that roots from our separation from the land, people sense that, people know that the whole earth is suffering—

FIRST GIRL. *(Overlapping.)* Because I couldn't go to the bathroom. And there's like nothing out there at all?

FIRST BOY. *(Overlapping.)* Will you please shut up? No one wants to hear about it!

VOICE #5. For National Public Radio—

VOICE #6. And peace on earth. For ABC news, this is—

(The voices fade out. The CHORUS members go back to presenting gifts to the buffalo.)

JOHN. I saw it all happen. In my mind. In a dream. I saw the father die, I saw the light, I didn't understand any of it. And so I'm here. I was the first. To know.

(Lights up on ABBY addressing an imaginary crowd.)

WHITE BUFFALO

ABBY. Okay, okay, can I have everybody's attention please? Can you form a single line, um... okay? *(She takes a question.)* No we can't have flash photography, all right? If you don't have a flash, you can take all the pictures you want—take 'em home, get 'em laminated, I don't care—she's sleeping right now, so if you could please be a little bit quiet—no—hey—you can't go past the fence, okay? The mother is very protective of the calf—she will... she will trample you down and that will be the end of peace on earth for you. We have some lemonade near the house if you're thirsty—it's twenty-five cents per cup, my Mom made it, lots of sugar, please keep it away from the kids.

(Lights fade on her. The phone rings. CAROL answers it as the lights switch to the kitchen.)

CAROL. No I'm sorry we don't have a website—we're hoping to get one soon—if you want directions can just punch in the name Gelling and Blackhawk—we're just south of town on County Highway B. Yep. Yep. No charge. Totally free. Thank you. *(She hangs up and gets about a step away from the phone before it rings again. She picks it up.)* Yes it is. Thank you. Thank you very much. Nope, come on down any time between eight and eight—right—right—*(She hangs up—the phone rings again.)* Hello? Yes it is. No, you can't camp on the property—I think there's a place just west of town— thank you.

(She hangs up. ABBY comes in through the screen door.)

ABBY. Jesus Christ—

(The phone rings.)

CAROL. Can you get that? I've got to get these brownies out of the oven.

ABBY. You're making brownies?

CAROL. Yes—just answer the phone.

(CAROL opens the oven as ABBY answers the phone.)

ABBY. Yes it is. Yeah, come on down. We got tons of white ones. Yep. Thirty. Whole herd. No I'm kidding, there's just one. Yes, please, open to everyone—

(She hangs up.)

CAROL. What do you think, twenty-five cents a brownie?

ABBY. Sure. *(The phone rings. ABBY grabs it. She speaks very quickly without waiting for a response.)* Come and see the miracle. Highway B. Just look for the cars.

CAROL. Can you run this lemonade out there?

ABBY. I'm running the next tour. *(Someone knocks at the front door. ABBY shouts at them.)* Just go around the side! Follow all the people! *(To CAROL.)* Goddamn it, we should charge admission.

CAROL. We're not charging admission. You know somebody called up today and offered to buy her for five thousand dollars.

ABBY. Ha.

CAROL. We could get a new car.

(The phone rings. ABBY picks it up.)

ABBY. Miracle. Highway B. Follow the cars.

(She hangs up.)

CAROL. You know, someone could be actually trying to call us.

ABBY. You answer the phone then.

CAROL. I will. *(They wait for a second, expecting it to ring.)* I was expecting it was gonna ring right then.

ABBY. Yeah. *(It rings. CAROL picks it up.)*

CAROL. Yes? Hello? This is. No I'm sorry my long-distance plan is just fine. No, take me off your list—

(ABBY grabs the phone from her.)

ABBY. Hey listen, buddy. We've just had a big fucking miracle down here, so there are a lot of very religious people trying to make pilgrimages to our back yard, so they need to have the phone lines open!

(She hangs up and laughs. CAROL laughs too.)

CAROL. I can't believe you did that.

ABBY. *(Still laughing.)* What? Those people get what they deserve.

CAROL. They're just doing a job.

ABBY. No no, I don't buy that. If you agree to work for a place, then you take responsibility for that company's actions. Those people could have gotten other jobs—

CAROL. All right. All right.

(ABBY sits down on the floor heavily.)

ABBY. What time is it?

CAROL. It's almost four.

ABBY. That's it?

CAROL. You need to go back out there.

ABBY. I know. *(ABBY starts getting up again.)* I'm just exhausted.

CAROL. It's all right.

(Pause.)

ABBY. You know there was a guy from Mexico City here today? He drove here. Can you believe that?

CAROL. I can do you better. You know who called today? Guess.

ABBY. No.

CAROL. The Dalai Lama.

(ABBY bursts out laughing.)

ABBY. You're a dirty liar.

CAROL. I'm serious, it was him.

ABBY. How do you know? Did you recognize his voice on the phone?!

CAROL. Who calls up and lies by saying they're the Dalai Lama?

ABBY. What did he want?

CAROL. He wanted to say hi. You know, congratulate us and stuff.

ABBY. You're such a liar.

CAROL. He said he might stop by.

ABBY. Are you serious?

CAROL. Yes!

(ABBY laughs.)

WHITE BUFFALO

ABBY. The Dalai Lama is coming here.

CAROL. If he can work it into his schedule.

(ABBY gives her mother a big enthusiastic hug.)

ABBY. This is so awesome. *(ABBY lets go of her and starts pacing.)* Oh I got some questions for him! I gotta write some things down!

CAROL. Well I don't know that he's going to have any time—

ABBY. Oh we're having a talk. Me and the Dalai Lama—you can go back brownies or make lemonade or whatever Martha Stuart stuff you wanna do, I'm gonna get some answers from this guy—

(She gives a little scream of excitement.)

CAROL. Isn't this the coolest thing in the world? Look—whatever happens, we're together on this, okay?

ABBY. All right.

CAROL. God this is cool!

ABBY. I know! Oh—I forgot, they're having a big pow-wow here Saturday night.

CAROL. Who's they?

ABBY. I think there's a shaman from the Lakota tribe, and there's a couple more from some other tribes, I'm not sure, and they're talking like—I don't know, maybe two hundred people. I told them they could use the fire pit out back near the Henderson's place.

CAROL. What?

ABBY. Yeah and they invited us too!

CAROL. Why didn't you ask me if they could have a pow-wow?

ABBY. What am I gonna say?

CAROL. You could say, 'I gotta check with my Mom.'

ABBY. Oh gee—sorry.

CAROL. How are we gonna have a party for two hundred people?

ABBY. 'Sorry, I'm not sure that you can celebrate the birth of the savior of the world, I have to clear that through my mother. Please put your religious ecstasy on hold until we get the OK from the administration.'

CAROL. I'm serious—do you even know what goes on at one of these things?

ABBY. I figure we're gonna smoke a lot of peyote and commune with nature. I think it's a way of becoming a herd—

CAROL. You are not—

ABBY. I'm joking. God, listen to you. It's a religious observance. You can't exactly tell them not to do it—And they invited us—

CAROL. You're not smoking any peace pipe at this thing.

ABBY. Mom.

CAROL. I don't know what you think's gonna happen—

ABBY. *(Overlapping.)* You're not grasping the significance of the event, okay?

CAROL. *(Overlapping.)* Oh I'm grasping it—

ABBY. *(Overlapping.)* This isn't a high school party! This isn't me going around hanging out with the "wrong" crowd! This is a historical event that we have been chosen—

CAROL. *(Overlapping.)* What do you mean "chosen"—

ABBY. *(Continuous.)* To participate in! And that doesn't mean baking brownies or making lemonade—it means participating—we can't sit here and make rules about what is and isn't acceptable in their religion, all right?

CAROL. Fine. I'm not trying to do that. I'm just saying if there's a bonfire and two hundred people on my land, I'm legally responsible for that. And if there's drug use or—

ABBY. Oh come on—

CAROL. What?

ABBY. Do you know what you sound like? You should enjoy this, you should be enthusiastic—

CAROL. You are not joining the Sioux Nation, I don't care if—

ABBY. Fine. Fine. Forget it. I'll tell them to rent out the VFW place downtown. And I'll stay in and watch TV.

(ABBY storms off. CAROL stands there for a second as the sound of drums is heard growing louder in the background. Lights fade as the drums continue to increase in volume. In the dark, a sudden burst of raucous energetic singing and the fierce pounding of drums punctuate the silence. The effect is thrilling, but also frightening.

Lights up on the "campsite." The CHORUS has created a ring around an imaginary fire. Each of them has a drum which they play with great vigor and speed. The FIRST MAN leads the singing, which is considerably different than previous songs. ABBY emerges cautiously from upstage, dressed in party clothes that are not entirely appropriate for the situation. She hesitates at the edge of visibility, a little bit afraid of the celebration. She watches for a second, then is about to back away before the FIRST MAN spots her. Without stopping his drumming, he motions for her to come and sit next to him. ABBY waves tentatively, but does not approach. The FIRST MAN motions again, but ABBY is still hesitant. Finally, the FIRST MAN stops his drumming, stands up, and guides ABBY to a seat. She sits down, waves a little bit to the other people there, and watches. The FIRST BOY lets out a particularly high-pitched keening noise, scaring ABBY more than a little. The FIRST MAN resumes his drumming, but soon holds up a hand to the others. They nod, and together they finish a hail of blows on their drums. ABBY looks around nervously.)

ABBY. Hi. *(No one says anything.)* Um... I was just stopping in—you don't have to stop or anything, I was gonna... um.. I'm gonna head back to the house and—

(She makes to get up, but the FIRST MAN stops her.)

FIRST MAN. Stay with us. *(He hands her his drum.)* We'd be honored if you would join in.
ABBY. Well I haven't really—I don't really know how—
FIRST MAN. It's very simple. Follow me.

(He plays a simple beat on the edge of the drum. He looks at her expectantly.)

ABBY. Okay. *(ABBY tries to play the same beat with him. She's not very good at it.)* I suck at this.
FIRST MAN. Yes. *(They both laugh.)* Relax. You're too self-conscious about it. *(He guides her hands to play the beat.)* Go limp. It's very easy. *(He continues to guide her hands for a moment, then lets her go and plays alongside her.)* Good.

(ABBY smiles. He plays with her for a few seconds before stopping. He motions for ABBY to continue to play. She plays alone, trying very hard to keep the beat. The FIRST MAN takes a step back and begins a slow, reverential song. ABBY tries as hard as she can, but it's difficult for her to keep the right beat. Seeing her difficulty, the FIRST GIRL helps out, keeping the beat with her. The song finishes.)

ABBY. What was that song about?

WHITE BUFFALO

FIRST MAN. It was a song to honor our Grandmother Earth. And to give thanks for her gifts. *(He stands up and speaks loudly and clearly in the Lakota language.)* White Buffalo Woman, we honor you. White Buffalo Woman, we thank you for the knowledge you have given us. We honor you.

(When he is finished, all members of the CHORUS begin to play their drums loudly and quickly. ABBY looks confused until the FIRST MAN sits next to her and plays. They all play together for a moment before the FIRST MAN lets out a high-pitched trill. After another series of beats, the FIRST WOMAN lets out the same noise. They take turns in the circle until clearly it is ABBY's turn to make the noise. She misses her moment, but they keep playing for her. She misses two or three more chances, looking around for support, until finally she attempts to make the same noise. She does a fairly good job of it, and the others smile and laugh in approval. Leaving the women to continue the beat, the FIRST MAN and FIRST BOY get up to dance. Each member of the group continues to trill as the men perform a ritualized dance around the center of the circle. They finish, and rejoin the drumming. The women get up next, with the FIRST GIRL pulling ABBY to her feet. They begin to dance as well, and after some prodding, ABBY attempts to imitate what they are doing. The FIRST GIRL takes a moment to show her the steps slowly, and ABBY begins to dance along with them. The dancing continues as the lights slowly fade. One by one, the CHORUS members vanish from sight, but we can still hear the sound of them drumming. Finally, ABBY is alone, dancing in her own pool of light. The sound of drumming begins to fade as the lights shift back to illuminate the yard. JOHN is there, standing against the fence. ABBY spots him and runs up to him as the sound from the drumming disappears entirely.)

ABBY. Hey!

(She gives him a big hug. He's clearly uncomfortable.)

JOHN. Hello.

ABBY. I thought you went back to Chicago.

JOHN. I came up for the pow-wow.

ABBY. Cool. Where were you, though? I didn't see you over there.

JOHN. I was out here, actually.

ABBY. Doin' what?

JOHN. Nothing. Did you enjoy the party?

ABBY. Yeah! Yeah—it was... incredible. Like an entirely new world, you know? *(ABBY takes out a cigarette.)* Have you seen my Mom around?

JOHN. No.

ABBY. Cool. You want one?

JOHN. No thanks.

ABBY. *(Referring to the brand of cigarette.)* Check it out: American Spirit.

JOHN. That's not really produced by native Americans you know. Just because there's a picture of one on the box doesn't really mean that it's any more natural or spiritual than Camel. And it's a little insulting that these corporations are profiting from exploiting my heritage in order to peddle a narcotic—but it's nice to see that you've bought into it. *(Pause.)* I'm totally kidding. I don't know who makes those things.

(He laughs. ABBY relaxes a little bit but doesn't join in.)

ABBY. Now I feel kinda weird about smoking it. *(Pause. ABBY*

WHITE BUFFALO

walks over to the fence.) This is so amazing, isn't it? *(No response.)*
How long have you been out here?

JOHN. A few hours.

ABBY. You didn't want to come over to the pow-wow?

JOHN. Didn't feel like it.

ABBY. That's too bad—it was... it was...

JOHN. I know what they are.

ABBY. So are you from Chicago originally?

JOHN. South Dakota.

ABBY. I bet that's fun.

(JOHN gives her an incredulous look.)

JOHN. Have you been to South Dakota?

(ABBY tries to laugh it off.)

ABBY. I'm kidding.

JOHN. I haven't been back there for a while.

ABBY. Yeah I wouldn't go back there either. I mean, I guess if
you're probably from there, it's probably different. What am I talking about? I'm from Po-Dunk Wisconsin. This place sucks.

JOHN. It's not so bad. At least it's quiet.

ABBY. Well when there aren't pow-wows going on it's quiet.
(She laughs.) I'm sorry, do I just keep saying things that are horribly
offensive?

JOHN. Don't worry about it.

ABBY. You know it's really cool to see everything around here...
transformed. And to take what had been ordinary and have it all...
mystical. I never thought this place would be worth anything.

JOHN. You've got an Arby's.

(She laughs.)

ABBY. Yeah, that gives us our distinctive smell. But seriously, this is like Raisinville. We're a town full of raisin people—people might start out juicy and full, but they get the life sucked out of them by living here until there's nothing left but these kind of withered husks who worry about clipping coupons for Cheez-its and living vicariously through the Green Bay Packers. It's sad. When I leave here, I'm out.

JOHN. I was the same way.

ABBY. Really? You have any family back there?

JOHN. My parents.

ABBY. You don't see them?

JOHN. Not too often.

ABBY. Got any brothers or sisters?

JOHN. I uh... had a brother... but he died.

ABBY. Oh. Mine too. *(She smiles at him.)* Younger or older?

JOHN. Older... He got hit by a car.

ABBY. I'm sorry. *(Pause. ABBY plays with some of the art.)* You know, just before Hope was born... I was out here with her father. Big Ralph. I originally named him Ralph, but, you know, he became Big Ralph... And... um... he was real sick—I mean he couldn't even really move, so I used to bring him water—And he would lie down in the shade over there—cause it was real hot—and I remember, the last day he was alive, I brought the pail out, and... there he was, just this great big shaggy hump, and his skin was tight against his ribs, and his breath was all shallow and ragged—You ever watch something die in front of you? At the end, he start spasming, and you could hear his bones—they were so dry you could actually hear them as he twisted around... and he let me touch him, and I held on to him—this huge animal—I felt so sad for him—cause I had felt the same way, you know?

WHITE BUFFALO

JOHN. Yeah.... My brother... was in a lot of pain... before he ever got hit.

ABBY. Sorry.

(JOHN walks toward the fence.)

JOHN. It's not so bad here.

ABBY. Give it a couple of days.

JOHN. I was actually thinking about... staying on nearby, taking some time off, just to... get my head together about this.

ABBY. You could be like our night watchman or something. I'm sure my Mom would go for it.

JOHN. Maybe.

ABBY. We could really use some help. I don't know if we can pay you much.

JOHN. It's all right.

ABBY. Great. So you need to get your head together, huh? Is that why you've been standing out here all night?

JOHN. It's just... this place reminds of home, that's all. In a strange way. Like you said, it's... transformed. Strange to see it.

ABBY. It's the unity thing, right?

JOHN. What?

ABBY. You know, the unity of all races. Peace on earth. You can see it right here.

JOHN. Well I don't know about that.

ABBY. But I mean isn't it possible that it's really happening? Think about it. This farm has become kind of a... union, you know? Like what you said happened in the prophecy.

JOHN. Maybe...

ABBY. It starts here. And it starts with us—and then it spreads out from there.

(Short pause.)

JOHN. Don't...

(He stops.)

ABBY. What?

JOHN. I was going to say that I don't think you should... let yourself get carried away. There are a lot of myths, and a lot of prophecies, and as far as I can tell, none of them have ever come true.

ABBY. You don't believe in it?

JOHN. That that is the white buffalo woman? That the legend is true, literally true? There was a spirit called the white buffalo woman who visited a thousand years ago and now has returned to bring peace on earth. That this is unequivocally going to happen? Walls falling down, thunderbolts from the sky, angels—are they real? Do you think there is a living intelligent spirit that lives—suffused—in every particle of the universe? Think about it. That's what these people are saying—that's what this is saying—man and nature are one—there are no differences between us—*(He heads over to the fence.)* Because I think you can't swallow this one bite at a time— you can't say, 'it's a symbol' you can't say, 'it represents a unity' You can't say that the legends are fables—I think if you're gonna believe, I mean really Believe—if you're gonna reap whatever benefit that gives you, you have to go the whole way. And to be honest with you, there's no way in this world that the whole way is true.

ABBY. Why not?

JOHN. How could it be? How could it be true?

ABBY. You don't think it's possible that there are things beyond our understanding?

JOHN. That's not what I'm saying. I'm saying, I don't believe

that the Great Spirit fashioned four people out of clay—I don't believe that foxes can talk—I don't believe that there was a woman
who could turn herself into a buffalo—and to sit here and suddenly
claim that the prophecy is fulfilled is a sham to me—that these people,
these revered elders and shamans and whoever else is suddenly jump-
ing on the Sioux bandwagon—these people are capitalizing on luck—
because peace on earth, however nice it is in theory, is not a white
animal away from coming to be. Okay? It takes more than that. It
takes—

ABBY. But wait, if people believe, if they take that meaning
from it—

JOHN. No, you don't understand—

ABBY. I'm just a kid, right?

JOHN. I didn't mean it like that—

ABBY. I'm just a white person, what would I know?

JOHN. That's not what I was saying and you know that.

ABBY. Seriously, though, what would I know about your culture?

JOHN. I'm just saying everyone around here is acting like peace
on earth is around the corner. And I just want you to be prepared if it
doesn't happen.

*(ABBY doesn't say anything. In the distance, the cries of celebration
can still be heard. Lights fade. Thunder and lightning. A few
nights later. Around midnight. Lights up dimly on the interior of
the house. MIKE, soaked to the bone and carrying a duffel bag,
arrives at the front door. He tries the doorbell, but again, it
doesn't work. He knocks heavily on the door. No answer. He
knocks again, insistently. Finally, he fishes in his pocket and
pulls out a key. He opens the door just as CAROL is coming
down the stairs, tying her robe.)*

CAROL. *(Calling out.)* Yeah, hold on—*(She stops, startled, when she sees the door open.)*

MIKE. Hi Carol. *(She doesn't say anything. MIKE takes her in.)* Sorry—I was getting soaked out here—I figured you woulda changed the locks.

CAROL. What the hell do you want?

MIKE. Well... it's a funny story... can I come in?

CAROL. No.

MIKE. It's pouring out here.

CAROL. So?

MIKE. All right. Um... So I was in my kitchen today... and uh... I had the TV on... and I wasn't looking at it, and I heard your voice. So I turned around, and there you were, on CNN, and there was our farm, and there was...

CAROL. You saw me on TV?

MIKE. Yeah... *(Short pause.)* So I kinda took that as a sign.

CAROL. Well take your sign, turn around, and get the hell out.

MIKE. Carol, come on—

CAROL. Are you kidding me? What the hell are you doing here?

MIKE. Well I came down to—

CAROL. You saw me on TV?

MIKE. Yeah it's all over. You had this big miracle or something.

CAROL. I don't even know where you live!

MIKE. Minneapolis. I'm just, you know, three hundred miles up the road—

CAROL. Minneapolis? You're in fucking Minneapolis?! You haven't had the decency to call or write in eight years and you're in Minneapolis?!

MIKE. I know, I know, I'm sorry—

CAROL. You're sorry?! What the—wait a minute—there's no money in this Mike.

WHITE BUFFALO

MIKE. I know, I know—

CAROL. In fact, it's costing me money.

MIKE. Okay.

CAROL. So don't come down here thinking you're gonna get rich.

MIKE. That's not why I'm here. Can I just step in?

CAROL. No—you can turn your car around and drive back to Minnesota—

MIKE. Well I got a little problem—

CAROL. What?

MIKE. My car doesn't handle very well in the rain, so I...

CAROL. Ah, Jesus Christ—

MIKE. So I'm in the ditch down the road.

CAROL. I'll call you a tow truck.

MIKE. I was hoping I could use the tractor.

CAROL. That's it, I'm calling the police.

MIKE. Hey, come on, I'm telling you the truth, you can go and check if you want—I'll pull the thing out myself—

CAROL. The tractor's not working.

MIKE. What's wrong with it?

CAROL. How the hell should I know? The engine doesn't catch.

MIKE. How long has it been like that?

CAROL. Six months.

MIKE. And you haven't had it looked at?

CAROL. Do I look like I've got a pile of money lying around here?

MIKE. Well I can—

CAROL. Mike. Get out.

MIKE. I was pretty good at fixing that thing—

CAROL. I don't care.

(She goes to shut the door on him.)

MIKE. Oh come on—wait wait—please, I came down here to see you—

CAROL. Well you saw me—

MIKE. I'm sorry, okay? I'm sorry. You know it's fine if you hate me, I can understand that, but you can't not care. Please.

(She looks at him.)

CAROL. Well get in out of the rain at least.

MIKE. Thanks.

(MIKE steps in. More thunder and lightning. The lights flicker..)

CAROL. Ah crap. It's bad enough we're taking on water in the basement—

MIKE. You got a leak in the basement?

CAROL. Yeah the whole goddamn house is falling apart! Are you happy?

MIKE. Why would I be happy about that?

CAROL. Take off your boots, you're getting mud everywhere.

(MIKE goes to sit down.)

MIKE. Sorry.

CAROL. Don't get the couch wet.

MIKE. Sorry. *(MIKE sits on the floor and starts taking off his boots.)* So... how's Abby?

CAROL. Oh—you remember we have a daughter! She's out.

MIKE. Out where?

CAROL. I don't know. Out. Out of my field of vision. That's about what I get.

WHITE BUFFALO

MIKE. Oh. She doing all right?
CAROL. You know...
MIKE. No I don't know, that's why I'm asking.
CAROL. She's uh... she's great.
MIKE. Good.

(Pause. MIKE spots ABBY's picture on the mantelpiece. He goes over to it.)

MIKE. She looks like my mother.

(Pause.)

CAROL. What are you doing here?
MIKE. I just came to see. I just wanted to see this thing. I promise I'll be gone tomorrow.
CAROL. Your promises don't carry a lot of water around here. *(Pause.)* You can sleep on the couch.
MIKE. Thanks.
CAROL. But I want you out of here tomorrow. Okay?
MIKE. All right.
CAROL. And maybe if it's not too much trouble you can explain to your daughter why you haven't bothered to speak to her in eight years. But I doubt she's going to be as nice to you as I am.
MIKE ...yeah. *(MIKE spots one of the pictures on the mantelpiece.)* You still got this?
CAROL. Yep. *(Pause. MIKE studies it.)* ...it's the only good one I got of Trevor.
MIKE. I lost mine. He's—four—in this?
CAROL. Yeah.

(Pause. MIKE puts it back on the counter.)

MIKE. *(A little choked up.)* So what's Abby doing next year?

CAROL. I don't know.

MIKE. She's not going to college?

CAROL. Well she got... she got in to Oberlin, but she screwed up her financial aid, so...

MIKE. What happened?

CAROL. Basically she decided she didn't want to go to high school anymore, so her grades went into the toilet for the last quarter—she had a big scholarship and then lost it, so... so no college. Right now I think she's planning on getting knocked up and living a life of squalor just to piss me off. Or I guess she's gonna experiment with a whole lotta drugs until it does permanent mental damage. Wow—maybe there is something you could talk to her about.

(MIKE sits down on the couch.)

MIKE. I'm clean.

CAROL. Let's get one thing straight: If you bring anything into my house—I mean, anything—I will drag you to the police station myself.

MIKE. I'm clean.

CAROL. I don't care what you say—all I care about is what you do. You don't have to lie to me.

MIKE. I'm done with it.

(She eyes him.)

CAROL. How long has it been?

MIKE. Two and a half years.

CAROL. Uh huh.

MIKE. So maybe I could talk to her about that.

CAROL. I don't think she's wanting to hear advice from you. *(Short pause.)* You're getting my couch wet.

MIKE. Sorry.

(He stands up.)

CAROL. I'll get you a towel. *(More thunder. CAROL goes to a hall closet and pulls out a towel.)* Here.

(She throws it at him.)

MIKE. Thanks. *(MIKE dries himself off.)* So how are you doing? *(CAROL stares at him.)* How are you doing—

CAROL. I heard you. I was trying to come up with the proper bitter response.

MIKE. Oh.

CAROL. I'm fine. I'm great.

MIKE. Good.

CAROL. So you're... you're clean? You have a job?

MIKE. Yeah.

CAROL. Doing what?

MIKE. I'm a mechanic.

CAROL. Right. Any illegitimate children out there?

MIKE. No.

CAROL. Any legitimate children?

MIKE. No I haven't gotten married or... anything like that. You haven't either, huh? *(CAROL gives him a wry smile.)* You still look good.

CAROL. Well you look like shit.

MIKE. Yeah, well—

CAROL. I like the hair though. It's nice. I didn't like that whole aging hippie thing that you were trying to pull off... it was horrible...

that little rat-tail that you had. Plugged up the drain every day—little circle of ratty, nasty hair, like you were trying to farm it to make some kind of bath animal. Every day I had to throw that in the toilet cause you were too much of a lazy slob to pick your own hair out of the drain—

MIKE. Okay, all right—

CAROL. Not very attractive.

MIKE. You used to like my long hair.

CAROL. Yeah when it was thick.

MIKE. Well—

CAROL. You know we found a wig the other day, maybe you could use it.

MIKE. Maybe. *(Pause. They look at each other.)* I uh... *(He trails off.)* I'm sorry. *(Pause.)* It's good to be home.

(CAROL looks at him.)

CAROL. I'm glad you're not dead.

(Pause. She leaves the room as lights fade. Slow chant from the CHORUS. Lights remain dimly on MIKE, inside the living room. MIKE sits on the couch for a moment, then gets up, moving around to examine the contents of the room. He goes over everything carefully and slowly, dwelling on some objects that seem to hold memories. Meanwhile, lights up faintly on JOHN, who is near the fence, holding a flashlight. He examines the artwork there, taking some of it off the wall, then carefully replacing it.)

FIRST MAN. In the dark winter of the world, she will return.

FIRST WOMAN. In a time of hunger and sadness, she will light the way.

FIRST BOY. She will bring us to ourselves.

WHITE BUFFALO

FIRST GIRL. She will make us anew.
FIRST MAN. We are her children.

(JOHN takes a piece of art off the wall and tosses it down violently. The CHORUS surrounds him.)

FIRST WOMAN. She sees you
FIRST BOY. *(Overlapping.)* She needs you
FIRST GIRL. *(Overlapping.)* You are here
FIRST MAN. *(Overlapping.)* You are this
FIRST WOMAN. *(Overlapping.)* This is all
FIRST GIRL. *(Overlapping.)* It is time
FIRST BOY. *(Overlapping.)* You are here
FIRST WOMAN. *(Overlapping.)* She sees you

(Short break—Lights go out quickly.)

FIRST GIRL. *(Overlapping.)* You are her.

(Lights come up quickly on the living room. Later that night. ABBY is sitting on the couch, staring forward, not looking at MIKE. MIKE hovers nearby, embarrassed and quiet. No one says anything for a while.)

MIKE. So did you have fun tonight? *(ABBY doesn't respond.)* You know you should really... tell your mother where you're going... cause she worries about you, you know? So I hear that you're getting into some stuff—you know and maybe we could talk about that and... *(ABBY looks at him and MIKE falls silent. She turns away again. Long pause. MIKE goes to touch ABBY on the shoulder. She avoids him, gets up, then heads quickly up the stairs. Lights down.)*

WHITE BUFFALO

(Lights up on the farm. Mid-afternoon. She avoids him, gets up, then heads quickly up the stairs. Lights down.
Lights up on the farm. Mid-afternoon. The CHORUS members, including JOHN and WILKES, are near the fence, placing more artwork on the wall. ABBY is in front of them, addressing them and a larger, imaginary crowd.)

ABBY. The White Buffalo Woman told the people that she would return in the form of a white female calf. When she was needed most. When there was a time without food when all the buffalo were gone. And this legend has been passed down among the Sioux, as well as many other tribes, for many generations and... *(MIKE joins the imaginary tour group.)* So even though she was absent for so long, she promised to return. She made a promise with her people... so... if you want to get a closer look you can go up to the fence— other tribes believe that the birth of a white buffalo calf signals a time of peace for the world... and a reconciliation between native Americans and white people. In fact, some point that this is a... healing for the massacre at Wounded Knee... which was at the end of the nineteenth century...*(MIKE begins to approach her.)* There's lemonade—we're gonna bring out some lemonade in a minute cause I know you're all thirsty. *(She tries to walk away from MIKE.)* What?

MIKE. This is all pretty amazing, huh?

ABBY. Yeah.

MIKE. So you've had a lot of visitors?

ABBY. We've had about three thousand people come through here.

MIKE. Wow. Well... you're doing a great job.

ABBY. I'm sorry, what? *(MIKE is about to repeat himself.)* Fuck you.

(ABBY marches back into the house, leaving MIKE there. The phone

rings, and before CAROL can pick it up, ABBY grabs it.)

ABBY. *(Into phone.)* We're open at eight! Come on by! *(She slams the receiver down and sits heavily in the chair. The phone rings again.)* Goddamn it.

CAROL. Abby could you please be civil on the phone?

ABBY. Fine. *(She picks up the phone and talks into it sweetly.)* Gelling residence. Yes, we have had a miracle birth, how nice of you to ask. Sure. We've got lots of visitors. We're just south of town. You know, stop by at three in the morning, that's the best time to visit.

(CAROL grabs the phone from her.)

CAROL. Sorry. No. Eight to eight. Sorry about that. *(She hangs up. ABBY storms off toward the living room.)* Get back in here. *(CAROL chases after her. In the midst of this, WILKES has detached himself from the crowd and cautiously approaches the screen door to the kitchen, holding what appears to be a bottle of champagne.)* Would you quit acting like a brat?

ABBY. Why is he here?

CAROL. He's leaving today.

ABBY. That's bullshit and you know it.

CAROL. Hey—*(WILKES knocks quietly on the screen door.)* Yes?

WILKES. Hello?

(CAROL heads back into the kitchen.)

CAROL. The tour's outside, okay? I think John is handling the next one.

WILKES. I was wondering if I could talk to you for a moment.

CAROL. This isn't a good time—
WILKES. Just a minute is all I need.
CAROL. Well.
WILKES. Just wanted to—

(He holds up a wrapped bottle of champagne.)

CAROL. All right, come on in.

(WILKES ENTERS through the screen door and extends his hand to her.)

WILKES. Anderson Wilkes, nice to meet ya.
CAROL. Carol Gelling.
WILKES. I just wanted to give you this little gift for all your hard work here.

(She takes the bottle as ABBY comes into the kitchen.)

CAROL. Thank you very much.
WILKES. Go ahead, you can unwrap it.
CAROL. All right. *(CAROL unwraps the fancy paper, revealing an inordinately expensive bottle of Dom Perignon.)* Wow.
WILKES. You know I think y'all are doin' just an amazing job with this here.
CAROL. Thank you. Thank you very much.
WILKES. I been following this particular myth my whole life.
CAROL. Really?
WILKES. Yep. So when I heard the news... Wow. You know? Wow.
CAROL. Well you're welcome to, you know, look around at the artwork and everything... talk to the people.

WILKES. Well thank you very much. There's just one little... I mean, I don't know that I even want to bring this up, but... I've got a ranch in Montana—thirty thousand acres—and I got a herd of about two thousand bison out there—

CAROL. Well we've got seven—

WILKES. I know, I know... I was wondering, though, if there was some way we could come to arrangement—cause I know it's tough to have all this here—

ABBY. It's not that tough.

WILKES. Right, right. But—what would you say if I offered to purchase the buffalo?

CAROL. I'd say she's not for sale.

WILKES. That's fair. That's fair. Forget I mentioned it then. I'll get out of your hair.

CAROL. Thank you for the champagne though.

WILKES. You enjoy it. Here's my card, in case you change your mind, and I'm just gonna... I'm just gonna put a ballpark figure on this for what I would be willing to spend, just in case—

CAROL. Sorry—

WILKES. Just in case. Give me a call if you change your mind.

CAROL. Thank you.

(CAROL takes the card.)

WILKES. You ladies have a nice day.

(He leaves.)

ABBY. Bye.
CAROL. Huh.

(Pause. CAROL looks at the card. She flips it over, smiling. Her

smile vanishes when she sees the number on the back.)

ABBY. What?
CAROL. He wants to pay us two million dollars.

(Pause. Lights down. End act one.)

ACT II

(During intermission, the CHORUS continues to place decorations on the wall. By the opening of act two, the entire expanse of the fence should be swallowed in artwork. Drumming in the darkness. Lights rise to an early morning sky. All four members of the CHORUS are on stage, flanking the now fully-decorated fence. MIKE is working on trying to fix the tractor. He has pulled apart the chassis and is going over the wires, looking for a loose connection. He attempts to turn the key in the ignition, but has no luck. Again, he tries to fix the wires. He looks out over the farm, and his eyes drift toward the fence. The CHORUS approaches him, speaking to each other.)

FIRST MAN. He remembers
FIRST WOMAN. He sees.
FIRST MAN. The air is cold.
FIRST WOMAN. His fingers numb with frost.
FIRST MAN. The edge of the world tilts away from him.
FIRST BOY. He stumbles
FIRST GIRL. He sees
FIRST WOMAN. He knows
FIRST BOY. He wants
FIRST WOMAN. He smells the wet promise of melting snow.
FIRST BOY. His eyes are dim
FIRST GIRL. The world is sharp

FIRST WOMAN. The sky is jagged and strange
FIRST MAN. He sees.

(MIKE gets off the tractor slowly. He begins to move toward the fence.)

FIRST MAN. He sees.

(Lights fade on MIKE, then rise quickly on the interior of the house. CAROL is on the phone in the living room. ABBY squirms impatiently nearby.)

CAROL. *(Into phone.)* Uh huh. Yeah. Yeah. I understand. It's just kind of a crazy thing, you know? So I just wanted to check. Right. Great. Thank you so much. You too.

(She hangs up.)

ABBY. Well?
CAROL. It's legitimate. The bank vouches for him.
ABBY. I can't believe you're even considering this.
CAROL. Abby—
ABBY. Who is this guy? What do we know about him? What does he even want the buffalo for?
CAROL. He's an enthusiast on the subject.
ABBY. That's what he says, I mean, do we know that for sure?
CAROL. Well I've been checking him out on the internet—
ABBY. And nothing is ever wrong or misleading on the internet! Let's sign up!

(MIKE ENTERS through the kitchen screen door. He hears them talking in the living room, but he waits in the kitchen, listening.)

WHITE BUFFALO

CAROL. Look, he gave me the number of his bank account—they vouched for him—I found all kinds of stuff on him on the web—I mean, it looks good. It looks great. He's a major contributor to museums all over the country—

ABBY. Well what does he want to do with her?

CAROL. He probably wants to do what we're doing. Put her out in a field and let people come visit—

ABBY. What if he wants to skin her, huh?

CAROL. Oh come on—

ABBY. Sell advertising or charge people or find some way to make all kinds of money from this. The next thing we know we'll see her as a pitch buffalo for Nike!

CAROL. You're being ridiculous.

ABBY. I mean, think about it, the messiah is going to be owned. Can you understand that? Do you understand what that means? Everything gets co-opted—This is something pure, something purely believed in by thousands and thousands of people, and they're going to take it, he's going to market it, he's—

CAROL. He just wants to put her in a field!

ABBY. This is exactly what has happened to the native Americans time and time again—the white people move in, and as soon as they smell a whiff of money from it, they take possession—

CAROL. You're a white person!

ABBY. They carve faces of their presidents on sacred ground—

CAROL. What are you talking about? We are not in a Disney movie! He is not the Bad Guy! Okay? Why can't you be excited about this?

ABBY. Are you crazy?

CAROL. This is a good thing—

ABBY. How can you even say that? This guy comes in—

CAROL. And offers us two million dollars?! How is that wrong?

Listen. Listen—You're getting your ideas from movies, okay? You're spinning all these wild paranoid stories about this—it is what it appears to be. He's a very rich man who is very interested in native American mythology—and maybe, who knows, maybe he is actually concerned about the safety of the buffalo. And he is going to help us out. This is going to change our lives. Is that so evil?

ABBY. If he were concerned about Hope's safety, he's give us money to buy a protective fence or something even if we didn't sell her. He'd help us, he wouldn't take her away. He wants her, Mom. I don't know why. Maybe he's going to lock her away—but I'm not paranoid here, I'm being smart. I don't like that guy, and I don't want his money.

CAROL. It's not up to you.

ABBY. Oh this is such bullshit.

CAROL. Hey.

ABBY. You said we were together on this—

CAROL. Abby—

ABBY. You said it—you said we were gonna make decisions together. And now you're treating me like a little kid.

CAROL. You don't understand—

ABBY. Just because I don't agree with you doesn't mean I don't understand.

CAROL. You understand, huh? I have been poor my whole life! And this money, this money puts you in school, it lets me sell the place, it lets me start over. It could change the entire direction of our lives.

ABBY. Maybe I don't want my direction changed—

CAROL. You got into college, you're going to go—you are too smart—

ABBY. *(Overlapping.)* Why are you trying to make these decisions for me—

CAROL. *(Overlapping.)* You are too smart to be stuck here!

WHITE BUFFALO

ABBY. Just because I don't go to college doesn't mean I have to be stuck living on the farm—

CAROL. *(Cutting her off.)* Abby! *(She takes a deep breath.)* Do you understand that I can't support myself with this farm? I'm double-mortgaged, I have so much debt I can't ever leave—and I can't survive here without you. If we sell the buffalo, there's enough money to get me out of debt and put you through Oberlin with room to spare. We would never have to worry again. And if I don't sell it, if I don't sell it—why—because I don't trust this guy, and then you can't go to school because of it? I don't care what you say, you're gonna resent me your whole life.

ABBY. If you don't sell her—

CAROL. What?

ABBY. Her. She's not an it.

(Pause.)

CAROL. It's a buffalo. Not a person.

ABBY. You don't know that.

CAROL. Is that what this is about? *(CAROL sighs deeply.)* She's just an animal, Abby. That's it. She just happens to be a different color.

ABBY. There's more to it than that.

CAROL. No there isn't.

ABBY. You used to believe in her—before they offered you this money, you used to believe—

CAROL. No I didn't.

ABBY. Yes you did.

CAROL. I believe she's a symbol. I believe it's neat that all these people see her as some sort of God—

ABBY. But you don't believe in her?

CAROL. What, that's she's gonna bring peace on Earth? Unity

to all mankind? Oh come on—don't be ridiculous.

ABBY. There's nothing ridiculous about it.

CAROL. You're telling me that that animal sitting in our field is going to bring peace on Earth? Over in the Middle East they're gonna hear about this and suddenly stop hating each other? *(Pause.)* This is—myth. This is—a story. It's a fable. It's not going to save us. And yeah, it's pretty cool that it's happening here, but this isn't going to change the world. But that two million dollars sure as hell would change ours.

ABBY. You have no soul.

CAROL. Oh Jesus Christ—

ABBY. Hey—you know Mom, you know what? Fuck you.

CAROL. Hey. Hey! You do not speak to me that way!

ABBY. You deserve to be spoken to that way because you will not acknowledge that other people have other beliefs! And those beliefs are worth protecting and we have a responsibility—

CAROL. I am not responsible for them! I am responsible for you!

ABBY. Fine!

CAROL. Fine!

ABBY. Fine!

CAROL. Fine!

(Pause. They stare at each other like gunfighters.)

ABBY. I'm going to go write some pretty scathing things in my journal!

CAROL. You go do that!

ABBY. And you know what, I'm calling the Dalai Llama and I'm going to tell him that you suck, and that there's no enlightenment in this house, so he doesn't need to bother showing up, cause you'd probably sell him too!

(ABBY storms toward the door.)

CAROL. You will thank me for this some day!

(ABBY stops.)

ABBY. *(Calmly and seriously.)* No. No. I won't.

(She leaves. CAROL kicks at the couch. MIKE approaches cautiously from the kitchen.)

MIKE. You did a good job with her. *(CAROL glares at him.)* You gotta respect the fact that she—
CAROL. *(Interrupting.)* You're not getting any of it. You don't have any right to it. I have ownership of the farm and all the live-stock on it—it's in the settlement. And I will see you in court and I will leave with your balls if you try to challenge me. The money is for her—
MIKE. I wasn't saying anything about that—
CAROL. And I really don't appreciate you lying around here and snooping in on conversations that don't concern you—this was between me and my daughter—
MIKE. Our daughter.
CAROL. My daughter, asshole. You lost the right to call her yours when you didn't so much as send a birthday card for eight years.

(Short pause.)

MIKE. I took a look at the tractor today. Your starter was fine—it was a... there was a loose connection from the battery... so I fixed that and I got it all charged up for ya. Should work now.

(Short pause.)

CAROL. *(Quietly.)* Thanks.
MIKE. And I can look at that leak in the basement later... tonight if you want.
CAROL. Okay.

(Pause. They sit there for a moment. CAROL can't quite bring herself to leave the room.)

MIKE. You know, when we bought this place it wasn't a trap.
CAROL. Well there were two of us then, weren't there?
MIKE. I'm just saying that... you know, there are ways of being happy without going to college. And maybe Abby... maybe there are even ways of being here—and being happy.
CAROL. What do you want?
MIKE. I'm just talking.
CAROL. Yeah, well... You don't know what it's like to be here alone. There's just so much—just to float, just to survive one day into the next. And I'm the one stuck with it—living here was your dream—
MIKE. It was our dream.
CAROL. Mine was to have you here with me. To have a family... To have kids and...

(Short pause.)

CAROL. *(Continued.)* Without you I am a slave to this place. I get up at dawn, I have to fix everything myself, my hands, look at my goddamn hands—they're so... hard and... thick and... this is me now—I work and I work and I work and it is never done because it is too much. And I'm tired of it. I'm weary, Mike. I don't want to be here any more. But I can't leave, because if I stop for one second, I'll drown—this place will drown me. So yeah—could I use two million dollars? Yeah. I could. *(Pause.)* Fuck. Look at me. I'm pretty much done. And I'm... I'm so sad my life turned out this way.

(Pause.)

    MIKE. *(Quietly.)* I'm sorry.

    CAROL. It's a little late for that.

    MIKE. For what it's worth, I never... imagined it like this either. *(No response.)* I want to make it better.

    CAROL. No. You've got nothing to give me, Mike. And I don't think you've got anything to give her either.

    MIKE. ...yeah. Maybe I shouldn't of come back. *(CAROL sits there impassively.)* By the way, you were right to put me in jail that one time. I was pretty pissed off at the time, but... straightened me out some. I was a mess... I mean, I was... you know, I died once, OD'd in a cornfield—my heart stopped on the way to the hospital— they told me later I was legally dead for four seconds—

    CAROL. Why are you telling me this?

    MIKE. I don't know. I just haven't been right—coming back here reminds me a little bit... of how it was—before—Trevor—

    CAROL. ...yeah.

    MIKE. And maybe that's why it's so hard to get rid of me. This place was the only good thing I ever done—hurts like hell to see it—*(Short pause.)* I never wanted to leave you.

    CAROL. *(Quietly.)* I know.

    MIKE. But you asked me if—

    CAROL. I didn't want to.

    MIKE. But it was for the best. I mean, I don't know, wasn't it?

CAROL. ...yeah.

MIKE. I was gonna come back when I got myself straightened out. It just... never happened. I was... I mean I had lost whole pieces out of myself—till I was just like an appetite and that was all that was left of me... I remember thinking at the time—I was in Nebraska in the summer—I was walking through the corn, tall corn, the leaves on my face; I used to go out there in the field to shoot up sometimes cause nobody'd bother me—and there I am, among the roots of these corn plants, and they're so green, they're like... this is Life—all around me, just... erupting out of the dry soil—and I can feel the air buzzing with the heat shining off the leaves, and I can smell the dirt and the hot air, and it goes in and I look up, and I see the sunlight shooting down through the tops of the plants... and I knew, as soon as I saw that, I knew that was it, I was dead, and I fell, and I thought... 'oh well.' *(Short pause.)* That's where I was in my life. Oh well. I figured I deserved it—for everything—for abandoning you guys, for still being alive, for being so damn weak... for letting Trevor die... And I guess I was lucky cause after I got out of the hospital the cops got me.

CAROL. You could've called us.

MIKE. And told you what?

CAROL. Anything. She was dying to hear from you.

MIKE. Yeah.

CAROL. So was I. Sometimes I'd be in bed, and I'd think I'd hear you in the driveway. Or when the wind was blowing and I could hear the door creak—just for a second I'd let myself believe you'd come back. And I'd lie there, feeling the chills all up and down me, and I'd wait as still as I could, almost as if I made any noise I'd break the spell and you'd be gone... so I'd wait there, frozen, listening... So long I did that. I just wanted to feel you next to me for once... just one more time... I had to be strong. For Abby, you know?

MIKE. You are strong. You're so much stronger than I ever was.

CAROL. Why didn't you call? I didn't even know if you were alive or dead—

MIKE. I was ashamed—

CAROL. I didn't care about that—

MIKE. I did. I was trying so hard to fix myself but I just couldn't... no matter what I did I couldn't do it... I thought you hated me.

CAROL. I didn't hate you. *(Short pause.)* I wanted you back. I always wanted you back.

MIKE. I'm here now.

CAROL. You're gonna leave again.

MIKE. I'll stay as long as you want me to.

(Quiet. They hold on to each other. Lights fade. A single flute. Night. The house is completely dark, but the clear sky is festooned with stars. JOHN sits alone on a small hillock overlooking the fence. A loud crashing noise breaks the silence. JOHN jumps up, grabs his flashlight, and shines his light around, revealing ABBY, more than a little bit drunk, climbing over the fence.)

JOHN. Abby!

(She stops.)

ABBY. Whoah!

JOHN. What are you doing?

ABBY. I was just gonna... I was gonna...

JOHN. This isn't a good idea. Come on out of there.

ABBY. I just wanted to watch her sleep in the dark.

JOHN. Her mother is liable to get angry with you.

ABBY. I know.

JOHN. Abby.

ABBY. Okay. *(She climbs back over the fence clumsily, knocking off some of the artwork.)* Whoops.

(She tries to put it back on.)

JOHN. Here.

(He takes it from her and affixes it to the fence. ABBY totters a little uneasily.)

ABBY. I figured you'd be in bed by now.
JOHN. Are you all right?
ABBY. I'm fine. *(She sits on the ground.)* What time is it?
JOHN. I don't know. Three.
ABBY. Jesus.

(ABBY rolls onto her back.)

JOHN. Abby. Abby.
ABBY. I can't lie on my back?
JOHN. There's uh... horse shit next to you.
ABBY. Oh!

(She moves.)

ABBY. This is what I like. No moon. Just stars. Isn't there going to be a meteor shower?
JOHN. You're drunk.
ABBY. I'm rich, John.
JOHN. You're drunk.
ABBY. Drunk and rich. Two million dollars. Right in my pocket. Right in my goddamn greedy little pocket. Isn't that just great?

WHITE BUFFALO

JOHN. Your mother is going to sell?

ABBY. The bitch.

JOHN. Abby.

ABBY. She's talking about college—and she's talking opportunity, and she's talking about the future... blah blah blah... and I just feel like hell. And I wanted to spend one last night with... I was gonna say God... *(She laughs a little bit.)* I mean, the White Buffalo Woman, right? One more night with Hope. I feel kinda bad that I named her that, cause now it's like, 'we're selling hope' and that's this big symbolic thing, you know? Like, are we destroying all the hope in our lives because we're, you know, grabbing the money?

JOHN. I don't think so.

ABBY. But... back to my original point... one more night with whatever. And all I can think about being out here... is... look at this... look what this brought into my life—all this... all this new stuff, and this beauty, and this like... all this amazing art and these people from all over the world came here to my back yard to see a miracle... isn't that awesome? I mean, we had this life before that was grey and dull and ruined, and all this magic just exploded into it... *(Short pause. ABBY is crying.)* And it's gonna leave us. We're gonna kick it out the door. For what? For money? How much is this worth? How much is it worth to come home and see the fence and see the people and see the miracle—all this joy in people's eyes to be at your house, you know, to be in your yard where you grew up, I mean, wow—who gets a chance to experience that? Nobody in the whole world except me. *(She sits up, crying. JOHN comes closer to her.)* Nobody in the whole world except me. I'm the only one. Why can't we... keep that...?

JOHN. It's all right.

ABBY. It seems like we're searching for something, and then... when we find it, when it appears it isn't... it isn't what?

JOHN. Maybe this isn't what we're looking for?

ABBY. But it is.

JOHN. You know this is a myth. If someone's willing to give you a ton of money for it, take it.

ABBY. How can you say that?

JOHN. Because...

ABBY. This is a miracle.

JOHN. Why?

ABBY. Because I believe in it. Why is everyone making that sound so stupid? I mean, if you don't care—

JOHN. I do care—

ABBY. Why are you still here then if it's just a myth? Why not just go home back to Chicago and go on like nothing happened?

JOHN. Abby.

ABBY. Seriously, what are you still doing here?

JOHN. I was in the area.

ABBY. Oh come on! You've stayed three weeks! You've stayed longer than any single person who's been here. You're been watching the buffalo day and night—you're full of shit.

JOHN. Because...

ABBY. Why stay? Why stay if it doesn't mean anything?

JOHN. I don't—I didn't say it didn't mean anything. I just said—I don't know. I guess I was just hoping I would see my Mom. *(Short pause.)* Figured she'd make the trip by now.

ABBY. Why don't you just go home? *(JOHN shakes his head.)* Okay.

(Pause.)

JOHN. Maybe I'm just curious to see what will happen here.

ABBY. You mean if we'll sell?

JOHN. I don't know. Maybe. You ought to go to bed.

ABBY. What time is it?

JOHN. Three fifteen.

ABBY. Screw it. It's early. *(ABBY heads over to the bench. Pause.)* When the birds start chirping, that's when you know you've been up too long. *(She leans back.)* Hey look, a shooting star. *(Short pause.)* So are you gonna sit out here all night?

JOHN. What else am I gonna do?

(She smiles at him, then beckons for him to come over.)

ABBY. You want some company?

(JOHN heads over and sits down.)

JOHN. Sure.

(ABBY leans back and looks at the sky.)

ABBY. There's always shooting stars in August. Just think, though. All that is is a tiny piece of rock burning up when it hits the atmosphere—like a bullet from space—and people used to think you could wish on them.

JOHN. Huh.

ABBY. White people at any rate. It's that 'greed-is-my-cultural-heritage' kind of thing. Always wanting something. Never happy with what they've got.

JOHN. And now you're happy?

ABBY. I've been happy since this happened. And it's a real long time since I could say something like that.

JOHN. That's good.

ABBY. Do the Sioux have any stories about shooting stars?

JOHN. Sure.

ABBY. Tell me one.

JOHN. All right, well... my grandfathers believed that shooting stars were balls of ice and rock traveling at extreme speeds throughout the solar system, usually in elliptical orbits around The Sun, which we called, great grandfather of helium fusion, because our myths said that at temperatures reaching one million degrees, hydrogen gas would—

ABBY. Shut up!

(ABBY punches playfully at him.)

JOHN. Why are you trying to destroy my heritage? We were very advanced. All right, all right, I do know one... this isn't Sioux exactly, but it's one I've heard.

ABBY. Uh huh.

JOHN. Okay... Before the horses came, when the world was young, there was a tribe that lived above the clouds, and they were known as the people of the sky. *(Slow flute music begins.)* And at night, every night, they traveled in the same path—*(The CHORUS, led by the FIRST MAN, emerges from upstage. Each member is now illuminated by a sharp light carried somewhere on their person. Lights fade slowly on JOHN, but we can still hear him narrating the story as the FIRST MAN plays his flute and walks solemnly.)* Making trails across the heavens. If you watch, every night you can see them walking, and these are our stars. But there was one star who was unhappy with their path across the sky. *(The FIRST BOY, last in line, plays his own flute, a much brighter and quicker tune, in sharp contrast to the FIRST MAN's. He grows increasingly frustrated with their pace.)* He was known as Na-Gah, and he was very brave, but very arrogant, for he was aware that he shone brighter than his elders, and yet still he was forced to walk behind them. *(The FIRST BOY continues to fight to get his music heard.)* So one day— *(The FIRST BOY turns away from his family—their lights are extinguished, and he is by himself. A rumble of drums is heard.)* He turned his back on his people and sought out the highest mountain, so that he might shine there forever. *(The FIRST BOY wanders until he finds the MOUNTAIN. [Played by the FIRST MAN.] The FIRST BOY sees it and tries to climb up, but he is cast off with a peal of drums.)* But the mountain was too high even for him, and although he tried *(The FIRST BOY tries again, but is again cast off.)* He could not scale its cliffs. Its precipices were too steep, and every day he was forced to return to the ground. He was ashamed for he knew that he sought only glory for himself, and not for others. But still he searched, until one day he found a crack in the surface of the mountain.

(The FIRST MAN opens his arms.)

JOHN. *(Continued.)* And before he could think better of it, he slipped inside and found a tunnel which led up through the rock. *(The FIRST BOY climbs through the man's arms.)* He climbed for days in darkness, never pausing, thinking only of the glory he would receive when he reached the top. *(Rhythmic drumming, getting steadily louder as the FIRST BOY continues to climb.)* And finally, after weeks of toil, he emerged at the peak. *(FIRST BOY lifts himself onto the FIRST MAN's shoulders, standing. The FIRST MAN then grabs hold of his feet and hoists him over his head. [This should take place within reach of a hanging bar or some other support that the boy can reach.] He grabs the bar in triumph as the drums pound loudly.)* Na-Gah looked around him, and saw the whole world spread out below, its forests, its yellow fields, its clear waters shining with his light. But he saw the ice and snow on dark mountain peaks, and the churning pits of clouds—and he shuddered at the sight of it, for the winds whipped him, and the darkness closed in, and in the cold night he desperately wished to come down. *(The MOUNTAIN exits, leaving the FIRST BOY hanging from the bar.)* But there was no way down, for the hole in the mountain had closed, and he was abandoned, solitary and frozen, on the highest peak of the world.

(The FIRST BOY hangs alone. All the rest of the stage is dark except for the light shining from him.) In his last act, he caused himself to shine so brightly that someone might find him, and he became the brightest star, which we know today as the North Star. *(The light coming from the FIRST BOY intensifies. The music of the sky people is heard again, and slowly the FIRST WOMAN and FIRST GIRL gather beneath him.)* And to this day, some of his family have been trying to rescue their prodigal brother. But the mountain is too high, and when they fall from its steep cliffs, when they drop, they make trails in the sky, not the slow, orderly trails of their people, but swift and momentary, until they are extinguished. *(Both the FIRST GIRL and FIRST WOMAN attempt to reach the FIRST BOY, but cannot. They drop away from him quickly, taking their lights with them.)* And these are shooting stars.

(The FIRST BOY remains, suspended and glowing for a moment, before his light fades out and the focus returns to JOHN and ABBY. The sad flute music of the people of the sky is heard for the duration of the scene.)

ABBY. That's sad.
JOHN. Sometimes they are.

(ABBY leans in and kisses him. JOHN hesitates for a moment, then kisses back. Lights fade as another shooting star crosses the stage. Daylight. ABBY is sitting in the same place where she was, alone this time. CAROL is coming out of the house with WILKES. CAROL has a contract in her hand.)

WILKES. I think you'll be pretty pleased with the arrangement.

WHITE BUFFALO

If you look in there in section two, my lawyer put a few riders in there... you know, some things just to uh... make it more equitable. There's a right to visit clause, a fair treatment clause, an access clause—which basically says that the buffalo has to be visible to the public and accessible during reasonable hours. And this is just a draft, really. If there's anything else you need to sort of... ease your mind, I guess, I can talk to my lawyer and we can put that in there. I want to do what's fair to you.

CAROL. *(Paging through it.)* Uh huh.

WILKES Now we are gonna have to register with the government.

CAROL. Why?

WILKES. Taxes. After you get a transaction over a certain amount, well, Uncle Sam likes to get his cut.

CAROL. Right.

WILKES. Like I said, anything in here you find objectionable or a problem, we can deal with it. You take a look at this, I'll come back tomorrow, and we can lock this down.

(They walk past ABBY. She eyes the man.)

ABBY. Hey.

CAROL. Mr. Wilkes, you remember Abby.

WILKES. Sure do. How you doin', pretty lady?

(ABBY doesn't shake his hand.)

CAROL. Abby believes you're part of a corporate conspiracy to steal the spiritual heritage of a... what is it—indigenous people for profit and gain. Do I have that right, honey?

ABBY. Well I also think you're a tool.

CAROL. That's great.

WILKES. Nah, it's all right. I want to put you at ease, okay? I'm part Cherokee myself and the last thing I want to do is to... to uh... to take something that is pure, like this symbol, and exploit it, I am here as a custodian, a caretaker. Now, if you want, I can take you down to a museum I've funded out near the Crazy Horse monument, you ever been there?

ABBY. No.

WILKES. And what I'm really doing here is preservation. Okay? We're gonna take the buffalo, and we're gonna have facilities for its protection, it's gonna have a nice field to hang out in, toys to play with, you know, the whole bit—a place to keep out of the rain—

ABBY. Don't talk down to me.

WILKES. I'm sorry?

ABBY. I'm not a kid.

(He laughs.)

WILKES. Well aren't you just a little ball of fire?

ABBY. You don't invest two million dollars in something without expecting a return on your money. All right? First of all, I don't think the concept of ownership can apply to a... religious event, okay? Because this is owned by the people that believe in it, not by you,

ABBY. *(Continued.)* not by Mom, and I bet, I'm willing to bet, that when somebody sues your ass for this, your little contract isn't going to hold up and—

CAROL. All right, all right, she gets fired up. Isn't that great?

ABBY. No if you—

WILKES. *(Cutting her off.)* Listen. I understand your concerns, okay? I don't want to see anything—now you just—

ABBY. *(Interrupting.)* You can't simply buy and sell faith—

WILKES. *(Talking over her.)* Let me talk for a second—I will be happy to discuss this with you at a later point—

WHITE BUFFALO

ABBY. Oh sure after you've got the contract signed.

CAROL. Abby, that is enough!

WILKES. No that's all right. What exactly is your concern here? Just... explain it to me.

ABBY. I don't think that you can purchase a religious event—

WILKES. Well, that's your opinion, isn't it? But the religious event is inside a living, breathing creature, which makes it technically property, doesn't it? So in the eyes of the law—

ABBY. Well I'm taking a philosophical point here—

WILKES. All right, well, I'm not gonna argue that with ya. Listen—I will take you to my ranch, you can see where the buffalo's gonna be, I will introduce you to the man who takes care of my herd—you can have full access to all that—

ABBY. No.

WILKES. You know I'm bein' more than fair here, if you guys don't want to do this, then...

CAROL. Abby doesn't speak for me, okay? Abby is just... go inside.

(Pause.)

ABBY. Bite me.

(ABBY walks off.)

CAROL. Oh God, I'm so sorry—

WILKES. It's perfectly fine, don't worry about it. It's nice to see she's so passionate about it. *(They approach the fence.)* Now this is just some wonderful art here. I don't know if we can work this out, but I would love to take some of this and um... put it in a safe environment, I don't know if that's possible—

CAROL. Absolutely.

(Lights fade on them. Crash of Cymbals. Tibetan horn sounds. Lights up on the DALAI LAMA [played by the FIRST MAN]. He is bathed in a golden light, and only he and a small section of the fence are visible. He moves slowly toward the fence, kneeling before it, and placing a blanket on the ground. He intones a barely audible prayer as sounds of a solemn chant are heard. Lights fade on him. A clear chime brings the lights up on the interior of the house. CAROL, ABBY, and the DALAI LAMA are sitting on the couch. He has presented them with a colorful scarf emblazoned with Tibetan poetry. Long pause.)

CAROL. Would you like some lemonade?

(Lights down. Later that evening. ABBY is at the kitchen table, writing furiously in a notebook. MIKE ENTERS from the living room. He sees her in the kitchen and knocks cautiously at the doorjam.)

MIKE. Can I come in?
ABBY. *(Not looking up.)* Free country.
MIKE. How're you doin'?
ABBY. How do you think I'm doing?
MIKE. That was pretty cool today, huh? *(No response.)* Never thought I'd see... you know, the exiled spiritual leader of Tibet... hanging out in the living room.
    ABBY. I'm still in shock that Mom gave him a discount on the lemonade.

(MIKE laughs a little bit.)

MIKE. What you working on there?

WHITE BUFFALO

ABBY. Nothing.
MIKE. Oh.

(Pause. She still won't look at him.)

ABBY. Do you mind? I'm kinda busy.
MIKE. Right. *(MIKE waits a bit at the doorway, unsure of what to say.)* You know, maybe when this is over... you could come visit me... sometime. Up in Minnesota. I could show you around.

(Pause.)

ABBY. Why would I want to do that?

(ABBY grabs her notebook, gets up, and leaves through the kitchen door. MIKE is still standing there. He waits there for a moment before CAROL comes skipping down the stairs, the Dalai Lama's scarf over her shoulders.)

CAROL. Did you see this thing?
MIKE. Yeah.
CAROL. Come here. Look at this.

(She takes the scarf off her shoulders and examines it as MIKE heads over.)

CAROL. I can't believe... I mean, I'm still like—are you kidding me? Look at this.
MIKE. That's pretty amazing.
CAROL. You know, when he called, I was like, 'yeah, right.' I didn't even know he was coming today. I look out and there's this convoy and... oh my God, the Dalai Freakin' Lama. I mean, we

marched for Tibet for godsakes.

MIKE. I know.

CAROL. You know what was funny, though? When he was here, all I could think about was Caddyshack. *(MIKE laughs.)* I know, he came in, and I just thought, *(BILL MURRAY from CADDYSHACK.)* 'Hey Lama, how's about a little something, you know, for the effort?' How does it go? 'I cannot pay you, but when you die, you will achieve nirvana. So I got that going for me...'

MIKE. 'Which is nice.'

(She laughs and hugs him.)

CAROL. *(Laughing.)* I'm going to hell.

MIKE. No no, you're going to achieve Nirvana.

CAROL. Right. Oh man... what a day, huh? *(She flops on the couch.)* It's like I won the lottery. Really, it is... incredible.

MIKE. So you're really gonna sell.

CAROL. Yeah. I'd be crazy not to.

MIKE. Well—

CAROL. Can we not talk about that? I've been going at it all day with Abby over this—she keeps on writing out little essays and reciting them to me whenever she gets the chance. *(MIKE chuckles.)* Yeah, it's real cute. It loses a little bit of its charm when she referred to Wilkes as an eco-terrorist with a rapacious desire to arrogate the spiritual needs of the Lakota. I don't even know what arrogate means. She's got that stupid little pocket thesaurus and she's issuing manifestos like the Communist party. I swear to God I thought she was going to try to get the Dalai Lama to sign some kind of petition against me.

MIKE. She's pretty smart.

CAROL. You should've seen some of the things she wrote in high school. I just wish she would channel that energy into something useful, you know? It's just a little much. And she's just, she's so... angry right now—

MIKE. She's eighteen. You were pretty much the same way.

CAROL. I don't know about that.

MIKE. I remember... You were the head of that committee in high school—what was it?

CAROL. It wasn't a committee, it was a club.

MIKE. What was it called?

CAROL. The Young Anarchists.

MIKE. See—

CAROL. Yeah, but we weren't serious about it or anything.

MIKE. You were dating that guy with the Mohawk—

CAROL. I was not dating him—

MIKE. This was the guy who used Elmer's Glue to hold the thing up—

CAROL. He did that once—And we didn't date, we were co-presidents of the Young Anarchists.

MIKE. Wait, wait. How can you be president of an anarchist club?

CAROL. Shut up.

MIKE. Does Abby know about this? Maybe I should go find some pictures—

CAROL. You will not.

MIKE. We used to have them in the basement—

CAROL. They were all destroyed in the flood—

MIKE. You're such a liar.

(MIKE tries to head for the basement, but CAROL gets in his way. MIKE tries to get past her, but she grabs him. Brief pause. MIKE leans in and kisses her passionately. They tumble backwards toward the couch, locked in the embrace. CAROL comes to her senses and breaks away from him.)

CAROL. Wait...
MIKE. Carol.

(MIKE tries to hold on to her shoulders.)

CAROL. ...I don't think we should be doing this.
MIKE. It's okay.
CAROL. No it's not. You don't just get to walk back in here...
MIKE. That's not what I'm trying to do.
CAROL. And if this is some kind of ploy—
MIKE. It's not. You know it's not.
CAROL. To get your hands on the money—
MIKE. Carol. It's not.
CAROL. Because I wouldn't make it through that, you know? So maybe you should just better get out of here before I find out the truth. *(Pause.)* I don't forgive you.
MIKE. Okay.
CAROL. *(Looking at him for the first time.)* I don't.
MIKE. Carol...

(Pause.)

MIKE. *(Quietly.)* I should go.

(Pause.)

CAROL. Yeah.

(After a short time, MIKE stands up. CAROL gets up with him. She reaches out her arms for a hug. He accepts, and they embrace tightly. MIKE separates just a little and places his forehead

against CAROL's.)

MIKE. You know, if it was twenty years ago, I'd say damn to-morrow. And all that matters is right here... and right now. And I wish that I could say something that would make all the years fall away and for us to be young again... *(Pause.)* I still love you. *(CAROL starts to cry.)* And I think...

CAROL. Don't. Mike. Just go.

(He lets go of her.)

MIKE. Okay. *(He backs away a little. Pause.)* Goodbye.
CAROL. Bye.

(MIKE leaves. Lights crossfade to the fence. Around sunset. JOHN is standing at the fence. ABBY is nearby with a camera in hand. She takes a flash picture.)

ABBY. All right, now take one of me.

(They switch places. JOHN takes the camera in his hand.)

JOHN. Say, 'as long as the rivers run and the sun shines, all lands west of County Highway B belong to the Lakota Sioux.'

(ABBY laughs and JOHN takes her picture. She comes over and punches him in the arm.)

ABBY. You're awful. I can't believe you're making jokes about that.

(She kisses him.)

JOHN. I am deeply sorry.

(He kisses her.)

ABBY. All right, all right, my Mom's gonna see.

JOHN. You don't think she'd approve?

ABBY. She doesn't approve of most things I do. Then again, I don't approve of most things she does, so there you go. Did you happen to meet that guy? Wilkes?

JOHN. I saw him.

ABBY. She's gonna sell. I can't believe it, she's going to go through with it.

JOHN. Well—

ABBY. You have to do something about this.

JOHN. What am I going to do?

ABBY. You have to talk to her about it, you have to convince her—

JOHN. It's not any really of my business.

ABBY. She's thinks I'm a kid. She won't listen to me. She's going to go and sell Hope and—

JOHN. Abby! It's okay.

ABBY. What do you mean it's okay? Don't you care? Don't you want to see her stay here?

JOHN. Of course I do.

ABBY. Then we have to do something. I know this is wrong. I know it's not ethical to go around profiting from other people's religious beliefs.

(JOHN chuckles a little bit.)

WHITE BUFFALO

JOHN. Yeah, that's never happened in human history.

ABBY. Well why don't we just put her up on EBay then? I mean, come on! As long as we're selling, let's put her up for auction and we'll just take the highest bid. Why should this guy have her? I bet we could push the price up even higher if we wanted to—so why sell now? It doesn't make any sense. Would it be right if we had an auction?

JOHN. She belongs to you.

ABBY. No, I don't buy that. She belongs to the people that believe in her. We're just caretakers, and there's a reason she was born here—and we have no right to mutilate that purpose by selling what was freely given. It's wrong. Every inch of me knows that this is wrong.

JOHN. Would it be the first time something wrong has happened?!

ABBY. Don't I have a responsibility to change then?! If injustice has been committed throughout history, then am I just supposed to throw up my hands and say, 'fuck everyone then.'? No. I have a brain, I have a conscience, and I'm going to do something about it. And you need to do something about it!

JOHN. I can't do anything more than—

ABBY. She will listen to you! This is your culture, these are your beliefs—

JOHN. This is not my belief! How many times do I have to tell you that?! You have this idiotic idea that just because I am Lakota, that I have some kind of spiritual connection to the land or to this or to that outdated mythology! Bullshit. Bullshit. You swallow lies, you swallow—you've got me mixed up in this multicultural fantasy of yours where you get to adopt the imagined spirituality of whatever race happens to pass through your door! We are not savages; I am not some kind of flute-playing, drum-pounding Indian that communes with my grandfather's spirits and goes out hunting with Running Bear and He-Who-Shits-in-Woods! I have nothing to do with this! You know who my people are, you know who these people are? My father was a drunk, my brother was a drunk—you go, go to a reservation, see how many mentally damaged people there are— see if you find a decent house that isn't a pile of boards nailed together, see if you find someone with pride, with work, with a future, who isn't beaten over the head with poverty and alcohol and failure—I had two friends commit suicide in high school, and out of my class, five graduated! Out of thirty! This is fun for you! This is romance! You get to fill up your imagination with our stories and our songs and all the rest of it, but I look here, and I see my goddamn brother dead on the roadside, face-down in his own sick, after some joy-riding idiots ran him over. And no one did a thing. No one did a thing because what was one more death, really? And why should we ruin the lives of four more kids when they're ruined enough as it is?

(Pause.)

ABBY. *(Softly, crying.)* ...I'm sorry...

(JOHN attacks the fence, tearing off artwork and tossing it behind him in rage.)

JOHN. So go ahead and make your art and tell your stories! The dead are all that matter! Our grandfathers and our great-grandfathers and all that history—promise them, ask them, see what advice they have for us! Go on! Go on! *(JOHN punches the fence viciously. He recoils in pain, sinking to the ground and holding his ruined hand. He sits in the wreckage for a moment before looking at ABBY.)* People will sell their belief for a loaf of bread if they're hungry enough.

(He winces and holds his hand.)

ABBY. Are you all right?
JOHN. *(Grimacing.)* I'm fine. *(Silence. JOHN calms down.)*
You know, it's not really your fault... I just... it's just frustrating
cause it's... maybe it's nobody's fault.
ABBY. I didn't know that about your brother—
JOHN. Yeah, well... you pass out in the street in the middle of
the night... bad things tend to happen. What really got me was that
they never tried to prosecute the kids, and that's kinda when I... I
had had enough, you know?
ABBY. And you haven't been back?

(JOHN shakes his head.)

JOHN. I graduated from high school, got a scholarship, and I
was gone.
ABBY. I didn't mean to... I'm sorry, I just don't know what to
do. No one will listen to me, and all I wanna do is... keep this. Maybe
that's wrong too, I don't know. I just think that it... bleeds the value
out of it, you know? And if all we think about is how to... feed
ourselves or how to get by, then... then what's the point of any of it?
There's gotta be something bigger than us. And this happening here,
I feel that it is part of something. You've seen the people coming in
here every day, they're coming from everywhere, just to get a look
at an animal—and that's like, they're not doing it to get by, they're
doing it because they're moved, they believe. And I believe too.
(Short pause.) And I wish you did.

*(Pause. ABBY leaves. JOHN remains there. Lights change on him.
The FIRST BOY, dressed in contemporary clothing, pokes his
head over the fence, looking down at JOHN.)*

FIRST BOY. *(As LEE.)* Thought I'd find you out here.
JOHN. Hey.

(The FIRST BOY climbs over the fence and jumps down next to JOHN.)

FIRST BOY. *(As LEE.)* What's up?
JOHN. Nothing.
FIRST BOY. *(As LEE.)* Loser. *(He punches him in the arm.)* Shouldn't you be in school?
JOHN. Probably.
FIRST BOY. *(As LEE.)* Yeah. Me too. *(He opens a can of beer and takes a long drink. He hands one to JOHN.)* So what are you doin' out here?
JOHN. Thinking.
FIRST BOY. *(As LEE.)* Yeah I can see how that would be a lot of fun for you. Man, you gotta lighten up. Life is short.
JOHN. It is?
FIRST BOY. *(As LEE.)* Trust me. Some day we'll all be dead. Until such time, beer is our friend.

(He takes another long drink.)

JOHN. Lee?
FIRST BOY. *(As LEE.)* Yeah?
JOHN. What are you doing here?
FIRST BOY. *(As LEE.)* Skipping. Screwing up. Getting drunk. Getting slow. Getting changed. Time moves on—John—and you've certainly moved on, haven't you? Certainly done your best to run and hide—hide behind a little fence where everything is safe... I don't know if I'd of done anything different but let me tell you this

much: I don't think I'm proud of you.

(He gets up. The FIRST WOMAN, [As MOTHER.] is heard off stage.)

FIRST WOMAN. *(MOTHER, calling.)* John? John are you out there again?

FIRST BOY. *(As LEE.)* You hear that? That's our mother. She's looking for you.

FIRST WOMAN. *(As MOTHER.)* John?

FIRST BOY. *(As LEE.)* She's waiting for you. Our mother waits.

JOHN. What do you want?

FIRST WOMAN. *(As MOTHER.)* You get in here right now.

FIRST BOY. *(As LEE.)* She wants you to come home.

JOHN. What do you want from me?

FIRST BOY. *(As LEE.)* I want you to make me not dead. Can you do that, John? *(Pause.)* Some day far from now you will join me here. And we shall once more be at peace. And we shall return to where we came from—to the land, which we never left. Because you and I are the same. And you are a part of everything around you—and this is you. And me. And all of us. You damage it, John. You damage me.

FIRST WOMAN. *(As MOTHER.)* John?

(The FIRST BOY climbs up the fence again and drops to the other side. Lights fade on JOHN.
Lights crossfade to the house. Morning. WILKES is in the living room with CAROL.)

WILKES. Right. Right. Well it's amazing when you think about it. This guy Kolczak—um I forget his last name—he's one of the main people involved with carving Mount Rushmore, and afterwards he feels so bad that he put this thing on sacred ground, he goes up to the Lakota, and he says, 'anything you want, I'll do.' So they come up with this plan: we want a Crazy Horse monument, and we want one so friggin' big that it's gonna make Rushmore look like it was made out of tinkertoys. So, Kolczak says, 'fine with me.' So they pick out an entire mountain, I mean an entire mountain and they're gonna carve not just his face, but they're gonna put his body, and they're gonna have him riding his horse. Kolczak works on it for forty years—he loses six vertebrae carrying stacks of dynamite up the mountain—he doesn't get paid a cent—he lives in a shack on top of the thing—the whole rest of his life he's blasting rock off of the mountain—he dies, this is seventy-nine I think, his wife takes it up, and seven of his kids keep working. And they're still working on the thing. They've been at it over sixty years—and you know how much they got done? His face. They got his face done. And his hand. And that's about it.

CAROL. Wow.

WILKES. But you think about it: There's a guy who sticks to his word. He promised these people something, and he's one of the only white men who ever kept to his word.

CAROL. So when are they going to have it done?

WILKES. It doesn't matter. You should go see this thing, though. Largest sculpture in the history of the world. It's gonna be a whole center of native American culture—we're gonna have a university—we're gonna have scholarships, museums, a place were native Americans can come and you know, find a way to give back. There's so little opportunity for education, especially on the reservations... I

(ABBY and JOHN come in through the kitchen.)

CAROL. So you think the white buffalo could be a part of that?

WILKES. Absolutely. If you have a center for cultural heritage, what better place could it be? *(WILKES spots JOHN and ABBY.)*

WHITE BUFFALO

Hey, how are ya? Anderson Wilkes. *(WILKES gets up and shakes hands with JOHN.)*

JOHN. John Two Rivers.

WILKES. Nice to meet ya. Abby, how are ya this morning?

ABBY. Peachy.

WLIKES. That's great. We're just sittin' here going over the contract, go ahead and take a look at it, see what you think.

CAROL. Well, Abby doesn't really have any say in the—

WILKES. I just want everybody to be happy, okay? And you know, I was thinking about what you said the other day, and I just want to make it clear to you that this is not about personal property. Okay? I'm not gonna take the white buffalo and... keep her for myself, I don't see a lot of value in that.

ABBY. What do you see value in?

WILKES. I see value in having the white buffalo open to all people, I see value in having it close to the center of the Sioux community, so people don't have to spend as much money to come to Wisconsin to see it, I see value in having it safe, so that some lunatic with a shotgun can't take a potshot at it—

JOHN. Do you think it's in a lot of danger here?

CAROL. John has been working as our security guard—

WILKES. I'm sure you do the best you can, but you never know. Some people are ignorant, some people are... you know, deranged. Who knows what could happen?

JOHN. Are you going to charge admission?

WILKES. Nah, I'm not gonna—

JOHN. Is that in the contract?

WILKES. I can put it in there if you'd like.

JOHN. I just don't think people should have to pay—

WILKES. That's not what I'm trying to do here.

JOHN. What are you trying to do?

WILKES. As I was explaining to Carol, ultimately, I'd love to have the white buffalo as part of the cultural center at the Crazy Horse Memorial. Perhaps you've heard of it.

(Pause. JOHN gives him an icy stare.)

JOHN. I've heard of it.

WILKES. Have you ever been out to visit?

JOHN. My family didn't have a lot of time for fieldtrips when I was growing up.

WILKES. You should go sometime, it's quite amazing what they're doing out there.

JOHN. I'm sure. And you want to put this in the center of it?

WILKES. Yes.

JOHN. Why?

WILKES. Like I said—

CAROL. I think John's just concerned that—

ABBY. *(Interrupting.)* Why are there merchandising rights?

WILKES. Hmm?

ABBY. Why are there merchandising rights in here?

WILKES. I think that's a standard rider that my lawyer put in— I don't even know half of what she put in there—

JOHN. Are you going to exploit this?

WILKES. I think that's going a little—

ABBY. Just do it. White Buffalo.

CAROL. Buffalo don't wear shoes, Abby. Who's going to buy—

ABBY. Yeah and horses don't play football either but that doesn't stop the beer companies from using them—

WILKES. Is there some specific concern you have here? I've done my best to try and make this as equitable as possible—merchandising rights are a standard part of any ownership contract—I mean I don't even think they need to be in there, me owning the buffalo implies those rights—I would not need anyone's permission to take something I own—

JOHN. You don't own it yet.

CAROL. Hey, all right, all right, come on—

WILKES. I'm being more than fair here—

JOHN. Why does it have to be owned? Why can't you just accept that some things simply are? You people have used the concept of ownership—

WILKES. Are we getting into that? Are we getting into that now?

JOHN. Own the land, own the trees, own the water—own everything that matters, buy and sell, that's all that we ever heard—

WILKES. Ah come off it! I'm part Cherokee myself—

JOHN. *(Overlapping.)* How much?

WILKES. We don't need to sit here and have the same stupid discussion—

JOHN. *(Overlapping.)* How much are you?!

WILKES. What does it matter?! Is my skin as red as yours? No. Who cares?

JOHN. Did you grow up on the reservation? Do you know—

WILKES. Why do you think I do this?! My grandmother died there! I'm trying to make this world better! What are you doing?

JOHN. The world is fine as it is—It doesn't need you coming in and rearranging it because its miracles aren't geographically convenient!

(CAROL gets in between them.)

CAROL. All right, all right, guys.

(WILKES steps forward.)

WILKES. *(Calmly, to JOHN.)* I believe in this. I believe in making this world better for Native Americans. I believe in giving them pride. Hope. It's a tough shake they've gotten—and I've done enough building in enough reservations all over this country to know that. And you can look up my record any day of the week: I'm not in this for profit. *(He takes a check out of his pocket and puts it on the table. He turns to CAROL.)* This is two million dollars. You can sell me the white buffalo or not—that's your choice. *(He extends his hand to JOHN, who doesn't take it.)* We're in this together. And it hurts me that you don't see that. *(Back to CAROL.)* I'll be waiting for your decision.

(He gets his things and goes. CAROL, JOHN, and ABBY are quiet for a moment.)

CAROL. John, I respect your beliefs, but—
JOHN. No offense Carol, but you don't know what my beliefs are. And you may own the animal, but it is only valuable because people believe in it. And no matter what you say, you have no right to sell their belief. *(Pause.)* Thank you for letting me be here.

(He walks out. ABBY waits a second, then follows. CAROL is left there in the living room, holding the check. Long pause while she considers it. While CAROL examines the check, the lights slowly fade out on the rest of the stage until she is left in her own dim spotlight. A slow drumbeat begins slowly. At first there is one drummer, then a second drummer joins in, intensifying the beat. A third, then a fourth drum are added. CAROL remains with the check. Light fades on CAROL as MIKE appears upstage, in his own light. He is inside the fence now, in the area where the buffalo live. The drumming ceases as he approaches a center point, takes out a child's boot, and drops it to the ground. He waits for a moment, then heads downstage, opening the gate

WHITE BUFFALO

in the fence and passing through. He shuts it carefully, and the lights evolve into an early evening sky over the farm. ABBY comes out of the house, sees him, and stops. She approaches cautiously.)

ABBY. I thought you were gone.

MIKE. I had to say goodbye.

ABBY. This time you had to say goodbye, huh?

MIKE. I'm sorry about that. *(No response.)* So did your Mom end up...?

ABBY. What?

(Short pause.)

ABBY. She hasn't cashed the check yet if that's what you're worried about.

MIKE. That's not it.

ABBY. Is that why you were back there? Gonna steal her?

MIKE. No.

ABBY. Then what were you doing back here?

MIKE. I was just thinking about this fence.

ABBY. I don't believe you.

MIKE. Did you know I built it?

ABBY. No I didn't know that.

MIKE. I did. This whole place was soybeans before we got here. It was my idea to get the bison. Figured it would be cool. So I built the fence to make it safe. Took over a month. *(Short pause.)* I loved doin' that. Getting up at five. Coming out here before breakfast, before anyone was up—just felt great to be up that early, you know? And I'd just work. Felt great. Felt like I was doin' something for myself, and for your Mom, and for you, even though you weren't born yet. To be on my land... and to work for myself... and be good at it. I miss that. Twenty years and it's still here. And look at it. A work of art. Holding a miracle safe.

(Pause.)

ABBY. Do you think I need something from you? *(Short pause.)*
MIKE. No I think you're doing great. Listen, what I was coming here to say—
ABBY. *(Interrupting.)* Stop. All right? Stop.
MIKE. Okay.
ABBY. I don't need any life lessons from you. I don't need you to say goodbye. I don't need you to come out here and tell me how great this place was when you first got here, and I sure as hell don't need you trying to say how proud you are of me that I turned out so great—and what I definitely don't want, more than anything else, is for you to be sneaking around here trying to find some way to get your hands on the buffalo—
MIKE. That's not why I'm—
ABBY. *(Cutting him off.)* I'm not finished. I don't want you here. You fucking bailed on this family. And I don't care what you said to Mom, or what you plan to do, you will never be my father. *(Pause. MIKE is about to say something.)* I don't want you to talk. I want you to go.
MIKE. I didn't come here for the buffalo— *(ABBY begins to leave.)* Abby. Please. Just give me a chance.

(She spins on him.)

ABBY. You want a chance, you want a fucking chance? How about giving me one? How bout giving this family one? Do you know what I went through?! To have my brother die and have my father skip town like we were poison? I was a mess, and to come home—

MIKE. No wait I can—

ABBY. No no no no! YOU LET ME SAY THIS! To come home and find you, my father, the one who is supposed to be an adult, to find you, up in that room... to have you... to see you on the ground... fucked-up out of your mind... half-dead, half-zombie—How I was supposed to understand what was going on? Mom wouldn't tell me— I thought maybe you were gonna die too, I didn't know—everything seemed so fragile, like the whole world could die at a touch— You understand? I'm never gonna forgive you. You fell apart. And you had no business falling apart... You were supposed to help... me, you were supposed to help us. That's what a father does. He doesn't go off and become a drug addict at the first sign of tragedy.

MIKE. I'm sorry.

(She laughs a little bit.)

ABBY. You're sorry. Fuck you.

(She walks away from him again.)

MIKE. I never stopped loving this family, Abby. I still do. I love you—and I love your mother, and I loved Trevor.

(She stops him with a finger.)

ABBY. Don't.

MIKE. I wish I coulda been around. I mean I don't think there's a thing in the world I wanted 'cept to watch you grow up.

ABBY. Then why didn't you?

(Pause.)

MIKE. There are some things that I'm not happy about... that I did. And... and I can't really go back and change any of that now. I'm not really asking you to forgive me, but maybe we could... you know... start over. Like new. *(Short pause.)* I guess the only thing I would say to you—

ABBY. *(Cutting him off coolly.)* You know—I used to wonder what was so wrong with me that my father didn't love me. And I wondered why my brother died—and I wondered why I didn't look right, I wondered why I didn't have any friends, and when I wasn't even thinking of any of those things I'd just start crying. Every day I'd do that. But then I worked at it real hard, and I'd say, 'you know what, I'm worth something', and every day I'd just work on that, you know? Convince myself I was worth something. That I wasn't a dog. That I wasn't a carcass. I spent years doing that. And you did that to me. So there isn't any "new".

(Pause. MIKE nods sadly.)

MIKE. Okay. Then I just wanted to say that I'm proud of you.
ABBY. I stopped caring about that. A long time ago.

(ABBY stares at him until he looks away. Satisfied, she leaves. Lights switch to the kitchen. Later. JOHN is in the living room with a packed suitcase. CAROL comes down the stairs)

CAROL. Oh. Didn't see you there.

(JOHN doesn't say anything.)

CAROL. Hey look... um... thank you so much for you help. We never would have been able to do this without you—I mean, we wouldn't have even known about it, so... I know that you're upset, that I'm going to sell, and if it were up to me, maybe I would just give her away and not sell at all, you know? But... I'm sorry it's not a perfect world. *(In the distance, the noise of a pow-wow can be heard.)* Guess they're having another pow-wow tonight, huh?

JOHN. Either that or they're going to burn down your farm. *(CAROL starts to head for the back, alarmed.)* I'm kidding. Goddamn. You people.

CAROL. Oh. So where are you off to now? Chicago?

JOHN. Eventually. I'm going to go home first.

CAROL. To South Dakota? *(He nods.)* That's good. You know I should probably give you some money for your work—

JOHN. No. It's okay.

CAROL. You sure?

JOHN. I sold one of my kidneys.

JOHN. *(Continued. CAROL tries to determine if this is a joke. She laughs tentatively.)* I'll be okay.

(ABBY ENTERS from the outside.)

ABBY. Hey.

CAROL. Sweetie, why don't you wash up, we're gonna get ready for dinner in a minute.

(ABBY doesn't move.)

CAROL. You all right?

ABBY. *(To JOHN.)* You didn't tell her?

JOHN. No—

ABBY. *(To JOHN.)* Can I talk to you in the other room?

CAROL. What's going on?

ABBY. Just... John and I need to...

*(She looks to him for help. With none forthcoming, she takes a deep
    breath.)*

CAROL. What is it?

ABBY. I don't want any of the money.

CAROL. Abby, come on—

ABBY. I'm not kidding. You can keep it, I don't care. You can
have it all for yourself.

CAROL. That's not why—

ABBY. You want out of this place just as bad as I do. Or did, I
guess, I don't know.

(ABBY takes out a piece of paper.)

ABBY. I wrote down some of my reasons this morning, so if
you want to look at this, it will kind of explain where I'm—

CAROL. I'm not reading that. Look at me. What is this about?

ABBY. Well all right, maybe I'll just—*(ABBY starts to read
from the paper.)* 'You may believe that the white buffalo is a symbol, that it is not a spirit, or the reincarnation of a spirit in the literal
sense. You may think that this is simply a genetic anomaly, a prod-
uct of random chance, but I believe that it doesn't matter. Ultimately—'

CAROL. We have gone over this, okay?

ABBY. 'Ultimately, the value of the white buffalo is based not
on whether or not it will change the world, but on the belief and the
lives of the people it touches—'

CAROL. Okay, fine, can you just—

ABBY. 'In this sense, the miracle is not the presence of the white
buffalo, but our belief in it—'

CAROL. All right—*(CAROL tries to snatch the paper out of*

WHITE BUFFALO

ABBY's hands—ABBY darts away.) Just talk to me, I don't care—

(ABBY continues to read while dodging her mother.)

ABBY. 'It has touched my life as well as those who visit it. It has changed our world, if not the world, the least we can do is respect and honor—" *(CAROL grabs the paper, ABBY fights for it, reading (now imaginary) words from it.)* 'And you can go to hell and kiss my white butt—'

CAROL. That is enough! *(She crumples it up.)* Just talk to me. What is your problem?

ABBY. I was telling you what my—

CAROL. I don't want an essay! I don't want something someone else wrote and stuck in your hand—

JOHN. Hey wait a—

ABBY. I wrote it.

CAROL. Fine, fine.

ABBY. You don't think I can figure things out for myself? I understand what's going on here— This is what I believe in, Mom. Me.

CAROL. And you're willing to give up your own education, you're willing to give up college to stay here... and do what? Or rather, you want both of us to give up our lives to this? This is two million dollars, Abby—

ABBY. I understand that.

CAROL. It's a new house, it's a new life, it's college for you—

ABBY. I don't want it. Not this way. Keep it.

CAROL. I'm not keeping it, half of it is for you—

ABBY. Well take my half and give it to charity, I don't care! I don't want to see a single goddamn cent from it.

CAROL. So you're going to throw away your whole life—

ABBY. How am I throwing away my life?!

CAROL. You won't have an education, you want have a place to stay, what are you going to do? Have you thought this through at all? You're going to become homeless or something idiotic on account of some stupid grudge—

ABBY. It's not about you! Do you understand that? I have nothing against you! But what you are doing is wrong, why won't you even listen to what I have to say?! You're so blinded by greed—

CAROL. I need this! It's not greed—

ABBY. You need two million dollars? All of it?

CAROL. John, do you mind? Maybe you should give us some time here alone, okay?

JOHN. If that's what—

ABBY. He's a part of this too.

CAROL. What do you mean by that?

ABBY. I'm not taking the money. And I don't want any part of your new house. So... so I'm gonna go with John... Out west. I'm eighteen, I can do what I want, you can't stop me... I'm serious, Mom. I want no part of this.

(Pause.)

CAROL. You would walk out?

ABBY. You're pushing me out.

CAROL. You would walk out on me. Well I guess you are kind of like your father.

ABBY. Mom I don't wanna go... but I will.

CAROL. You have no idea what it's like, kid. You know it's nice to have these ideals—it's nice to have the luxury of believing in things. It's nice to say I don't need money. But you can only say that cause I slaved for you. I spent my life here. For you.

(Pause.)

WHITE BUFFALO

ABBY. *(Weakening.)* Selling the buffalo is wrong.

CAROL. Is it? Are we killing it? Are we exploiting it? Are we charging admission? Are we doing any of those things? We've done our best here. Okay? I mean, yeah, I admit it, this is a wonderful thing. I loved having all these people come and visit—and you know, the Dalai Lama came, and that's great, that's one of the best experiences of my life, and I'm so glad that you were here to share it with me, but... You have to be a little bit practical about this. Our lives are worth something too.

ABBY. Mom... This was the best time of my life. I was a part of something important—more important than our lives. And it doesn't matter how much money there is, it's still wrong. *(Short pause.)* I'm gonna go pack.

CAROL. You're leaving tonight?

(ABBY heads for the stairs.)

ABBY. I'm not gonna stay here and watch you do this.

CAROL. Wait a minute! *(ABBY doesn't stop. She heads up the stairs.)* Abby! *(CAROL makes a movement to follow ABBY up the stairs, but turns on JOHN instead.)* You did this. I don't know how, but you did this. Get out of my house.

JOHN. *(Calmly.)* Carol. Don't sell.

CAROL. Get the hell out of my house.

(JOHN waits for a second, then leaves. CAROL watches him go, then collapses on the couch. Music. The FIRST MAN appears center stage.)

FIRST MAN. In the days before the horses, there was a time of great suffering and famine. All the waters of the earth had dried, and the people grew lean and hungry. Under the fierce sun they toiled, searching the barren land for any sign of food.

(CAROL remains huddled on the couch in the fetal position as the FIRST MAN speaks. Near the end of his line, MIKE appears at the screen door, looking in.)

MIKE. Carol?

(She doesn't respond to him. He cautiously opens the door and ENTERS the kitchen, his eyes fixed on the living room. He stands in the doorway, watching for a moment before she notices his presence.)

CAROL. *(Not really looking at him.)* Couldn't stay away, huh? *(Short pause.)* She's leaving.
MIKE. Oh.
CAROL. Did you have something to do with that?
MIKE. How could I?
CAROL. I'm sorry, my head's spinning. I feel like everyone's against me all of a sudden. I just—I didn't think that...
MIKE. I'm sorry.

(CAROL gets up off the couch.)

CAROL. I got a real small family, Mike. It's just me and her. And now she's gonna go. The last one. One by one they go. *(MIKE draws closer to her.)* I don't know why.
CAROL. *(Continued. He touches her.)* It was good once, wasn't it? What we had?
MIKE. Yeah.

WHITE BUFFALO

(CAROL pulls away from him and heads into the kitchen.)

CAROL. She's listening to these people, she's getting sucked in by them—

MIKE. Maybe she just believes.

CAROL. Don't be ridiculous.

MIKE. She thinks for herself, Carol. I've talked to her enough to know that much—

CAROL. She's a kid, as much as she might pretend otherwise, she's a kid, and you know that if you spent more than ten minutes with her—

MIKE. Maybe she believes there's a reason the calf was born here.

CAROL. Do you believe that? That there's a reason?

MIKE. ...yeah. I do.

CAROL. Ah come on—

MIKE. I believe it.

CAROL. Are you kidding me? Don't you think it's a little more likely that there is a very rare gene that sometimes turns a buffalo a different color? I mean, this isn't the hand of God here.

MIKE. You don't know that.

CAROL. I don't know that? Are you serious? Look around this goddamn place! *(CAROL storms out the screen door into the yard— Mike follows.)* The foundation is leaking, the fields are empty, nothing works, the whole place is falling apart! And I'm supposed to stay here? Look at our lives. None of this makes any sense to me— you, Trevor, Abby, my life, this ruin... I don't see God shining in through the rafters here.

(Lights dim slightly on them as the FIRST BOY appears far stage left.)

WHITE BUFFALO

FIRST BOY. Two young men, brothers, went out to hunt. *(ABBY comes down the stairs in the house, lugging two large suitcases behind her. JOHN waits for her at the door.)* And they ranged far and wide under the sky, but there was no food. Their stomachs were empty, and they despaired.

(ABBY gets to the bottom of the stairs and meets JOHN.)

JOHN. That's all you're taking?
ABBY. ...yeah.
JOHN. You sure you want to do this?

(ABBY nods.)

ABBY. Don't you think this is the only thing?
JOHN. I don't know. I guess I just don't want you... to never come back, that's all.
ABBY. Well if she sells the house... *(Short pause.)* I suppose I should probably go say goodbye.

(Lights dim slightly on them as the FIRST GIRL appears far stage right.)

FIRST GIRL. And on the third day they met the most beautiful woman they had ever seen. She was dressed all in white, and her eyes were deep and black—
FIRST BOY. One brother—
FIRST GIRL. Knew lust in his heart, and he reached out to possess her. But he was consumed by the air
FIRST MAN. *(On "consumed".)* Devoured—
FIRST GIRL. Until nothing remained
FIRST BOY. But bones.

WHITE BUFFALO

(Lights switch back to CAROL and MIKE.)

CAROL. It's real nice that you can come back here and start believing in prophecies, but I can't do that. And I find it funny that you believe in all this forgiveness and salvation when you're the one who ruined everything in the first place.

MIKE. That's not true—

CAROL. It is true—

MIKE. Not all of it—

CAROL. You left us here to rot in the mess that you made! You sold my car, you sold my mother's china, you took and robbed every single cent out of this house, and I let you, I let you, I tried to be understanding as you snuck off in the middle of the night to Chicago to do God-knows-what so you could get your hands on that shit—because I knew you were in pain, but that doesn't give you the right to turn this goddamn house into a coffin and shoot yourself full of madness—why do you think I'm mortgaged all to hell—why do you think I can't send our daughter to school—and I know you blamed yourself... for him, and you should, but still... still—

MIKE. No! You can't heap all the blame on me forever! I'll take some of it, sure, I know I was a mess, I know I failed in so many ways, but you blamed me for Trevor, and that was not my fault! I know that now! I let you needle me about that, I let you stare at me, I let you pull me down with it! But you never let go! You never let me go! And you never—

CAROL. So you turn to drugs?! You turn to ruining your family and—

MIKE. That was a mistake! I accept that and I understand that, but Trevor was not my fault.

CAROL. Who's fault, then?

MIKE. Nobody's. I understand that now.

FIRST MAN. To the other, who showed no desire, she said
FIRST GIRL. Go back to your people. Tell them I am coming.
FIRST BOY. They need fear no longer
FIRST GIRL. And you shall become a prayer on this earth.

(ABBY approaches the screen door in the kitchen, but she hears her parents and stops, listening.)

MIKE. I remember... I was standing right here, it was January, when he was four—And I was looking out over the field...

(CAROL turns away a little bit.)

CAROL. Mike...
MIKE. I need to tell you this. And I was thinking about how beautiful it was covered waist-deep in snow. Like the old land had been forgotten, cleaned, and there it lay, untracked and rounded. And I just took it all in, breathing in the air that was cold like steel, like I was the only person in the universe who really saw it. And I was out working on the shed and Trevor was playing and I hadn't heard from him in a while—so I went to check, and I saw his tracks leading away from the house, a stumbling line of footprints in the clean snow.
CAROL. Please...
MIKE. When I found him... he was only about a hundred feet from the house—I thought he had just lost a boot... He had those little red boots... with the lightning bolts on 'em—and I went over to pick it out of the snow... but it was heavy... and it was wet, and I knew. He just loved to tunnel in the snow—I didn't think anything of it cause I did the same thing when I was a kid—I showed him how to do it—I'd burrow in... make a cave for myself where it was warm... and protected—a kind of secret world where you could go

and be safe... *(Short pause.)* Such a quiet way to go. I didn't hear a thing... the snow just fell in on him... and he didn't have the strength to pull himself... out of it... You know there are so many ways you try and protect the kid, so many things you try and warn him about... you try and tell him everything, but then the... the only thing you forgot... cause it wouldn't seem like... I mean, how could that kill you? It's snow... *(Pause. CAROL is crying.)* I pulled on his boot— but I couldn't get him out—he was in a drift... there was so much snow on him—and I remember screaming, but it was so quiet out, muffled by all that snow... and I remember it started to snow, as if in response—and you weren't there—you were subbing in the schools—I was the only one home—I kept pulling, I kept tugging on his boot, but I couldn't move him, so I got on my hands and knees and I dug with my hands—and my fingers were shaking and I clawed at it until I couldn't feel them any more until I finally pulled him out... his eyes open... he was so heavy... for being such a little thing... and I stumbled back to the house with him in my arms—and I tripped, and I dropped him in the snow, and I thought that was it, maybe it I hadn't a done that, if I coulda... it was too late.

FIRST MAN. And she taught us all the she knew

FIRST BOY. So that we need not hunger or fear

FIRST GIRL. But soon it came time for her to depart

MIKE. I tried so hard Carol. I held him to me the whole time I was waiting for the ambulance—he was cold... and damp... and I just kept hoping—

FIRST MAN. And as she left

FIRST GIRL. She transformed into a beautiful buffalo

FIRST BOY. Pure white

FIRST MAN. And she said

MIKE. I want you to forgive me. I forgave myself, I finally did. I was so gone for so long—but I'm back—

FIRST MAN. When I am needed most

WHITE BUFFALO

FIRST BOY. In a time of darkness and sorrow
FIRST GIRL. I will return
MIKE. And I saw this. I saw the fence that I built, I see the spot where it happened, and I look out—
FIRST MAN. And my sign
FIRST GIRL. My sign

(A white light begins to glow from behind the fence.)

MIKE. I see the same color white
FIRST BOY. Will be the birth
FIRST MAN. Of a white buffalo calf
MIKE. It's the same as the snow in my hands. *(ABBY steps out from where she has been waiting now.)* This is not a coincidence. *(ABBY approaches. The white light continues to intensify.)* This is from him. This is for him. It makes sense to me.

(The CHORUS members move from the cardinal points of the stage and begin to converge on the family.)

MIKE. That's him out there... We can't turn that out. That's our boy.
CAROL. Is it?
MIKE. Yes. That's him.
CAROL. I see—
MIKE Don't you see it?

(The CHORUS members surround the complete family now. Out of the light emerges the WHITE BUFFALO WOMAN, dressed in a scintillating coat of pure white. She is raised above them.)

CAROL. *(Quietly.)* Yes...

MIKE. Do you see?

(CAROL steps back and gazes up at the WHITE BUFFALO WOMAN. Lights fade out. End of Play.)

WHITE BUFFALO

PROPERTY LIST

ACT ONE

Wrecked and water-damaged boxes, containing:
    children's clothes
    clothing from the 1970s, including an outrageous disco shirt
    wig

Water Bucket (Carol)
Musical instruments: (Chorus Members)
    Flute
    Four drums

Newspaper (John)
Brownies (Carol)
Pack of American Spirit cigarettes and lighter (Abby)
Native American artwork (Chorus Members)
Duffel bag (Mike)

ACT TWO

Flashlight (John)
Contract (Carol)
Child's Boots (Mike)
Suitcases (Abby and John)
Camera (Abby)
Journal (Abby)
Richly embroidered scarf (First Man, later Carol)